Where
Have You
Been?

Where Have You Been?

Tank Crawford

WHERE HAVE YOU BEEN?

This is a work of fiction. All of the characters, names, incidents, organizations, and dialogue in this novel are either the products of the author's imagination or are used fictitiously.

iUniverse books may be ordered through booksellers or by contacting:

iUniverse
1663 Liberty Drive
Bloomington, IN 47403
www.iuniverse.com
1-800-Authors (1-800-288-4677)

Because of the dynamic nature of the Internet, any web addresses or links contained in this book may have changed since publication and may no longer be valid. The views expressed in this work are solely those of the author and do not necessarily reflect the views of the publisher, and the publisher hereby disclaims any responsibility for them.

Any people depicted in stock imagery provided by Getty Images are models, and such images are being used for illustrative purposes only. Certain stock imagery © Getty Images.

Illustrations by Cheryl Plunkett Mikula. Cheryl is an artist and art teacher for the Strongsville public schools and has been a life long friend of the author.

ISBN: 978-1-5320-9195-7 (sc)
ISBN: 978-1-5320-9201-5 (e)

Library of Congress Control Number: 2020900435

Print information available on the last page.

iUniverse rev. date: 01/14/2020

Contents

Introduction vii
Prologue ix

One   A Nice White Bow 1
Two   A Short, Round Man with Rosy
        Cheeks 9
Three   I Can't Believe It! 15
Four   Maiden Ride 21
Five   Meet the Gang 27
Six   My First Summer 35
Seven   Let's Race! 41
Eight   The Race 47
Nine   The Finish 53
Ten   Girls 61
Eleven   Meet the Girls 65
Twelve   The First Wreck, How Sweet
        It Was 71
Thirteen   The Apology 83
Fourteen   The Camping Trips 87

Fifteen The County Fair 95

Sixteen Middle School and the
Awkward Years...........................105

Seventeen Some Major Awkward Moments...109

Eighteen High School...............................117

Nineteen High School Ups and Downs 129

Twenty College! Go Team!.......................133

Twenty-One College is Over...........................137

Twenty-Two My Last Ride, and I Didn't
Even Know It..............................139

Twenty-Three The Cleanup..............................147

Twenty-Four Where Are We Going?.................153

Twenty-Five A New "Old" Friend....................157

Twenty-Six My Second First Ride.................159

Introduction

THIS IS A FICTIONAL STORY. None of the accounts reflect any living or real persons. Locations are fictitious.

It's longer than a short story. It contains about 34,500 words.

It centers on the existence/life of an old bicycle, seen through the eyes of the bicycle itself.

It also follows some of the experiences of its young owner's life as he grows from the eight-year-old-boy who received the bike for Christmas to the young man who finishes college and moves on.

All throughout his childhood, the boy and his friends enjoy the experiences and childhood activities that include riding their bikes.

These stories include the boy's first romance in high school.

After the college years, the bike is put into the garage for storage (more like abandoned) to languish for years, rusting and being neglected. And the bike feels it will end up on the curb as trash.

Then a teenage boy and his friend find him when asked to clean up the garage as a service project for an elderly woman. She tells the boys to take what they want as long as it goes to a good home. The boy ends up giving the bike to his father, who has been looking for a bike just like this one for years.

Finally, the story goes into how this middle-aged man restores the bike and gives it a brand-new outlook on the future and how this old bike makes this man feel young again.

It is basically a story more about the "life and times" of the boy and bicycle seen through the bike's perspective and narrated by the bike itself.

Prologue

Where Have You Been?

F OR WHAT SEEMS LIKE AN eternity, I have existed only in this dusty, drafty, creaky, old garage. Languishing in this one spot, I haven't budged in ages. I am leaning far to one side and am piled up with a lot of my longtime garage companions. I have become rusty, layered with dust, and tarnished in the damp garage air and have fallen into a sad state of disrepair. I wear a thick coat of dust and cobwebs accumulated from years of idle neglect. Certain parts of me no longer work, and I am afraid I will eventually end up at the curb on trash day like so many other things in this garage that have gone on before me. My owner has grown up and moved away, and his mother is elderly and alone now. She seems to have no desire or energy to ever use me again or at least have me fixed up. She lacks the ability to repair me, and I fear she no longer recalls many of the amazing memories I have of this family and my time here.

I cannot help but think that this isn't how it's supposed to be! I'm supposed to be used and cleaned and waxed to a high gloss. I'm supposed to shine better than anything around me. I'm supposed to be part of someone who is just learning what life is about, and I'm to be used to explore places never before seen by that person.

I had once been used to seeing his friends and being bragged about. I remember hearing them saying they wished they were lucky enough have me. We would go from one side of town to the other, and I would listen to tales from his childhood as he grew into adulthood and how I was an important part of his life. I should have been passed down to his children, so I could be part of their childhood, too, and part of their new discoveries.

Instead, I am rusting away, paint chipping, not functioning as I was designed to be. I am sad and fearful of what my future might be. It is dreadful to even ponder what the future may hold for me. How did I get to this place and in this condition? Oh, but what amazing times I have had. My history is full of excitement, daring, and wonder, and I have been to places that many people and my own kind will never see. I have had an awesome existence until these past twenty-five or thirty sad years.

A Nice White Bow

MY STORY STARTS A LONG, long, long time ago—over half a century! I can't believe it. Let me tell you all of it from the beginning, or at least as much as I can recall—how I was a special part of somebody's life. From the beginning, let me tell you *where I have been.*

It was late on Christmas Eve 1961. Snow was falling, it was bitterly cold, and the wind was howling around the outside of the garage. With an earsplitting creak, a large door swung open. I could feel the biting cold air, and snow swirled into the garage and onto the garage floor. There was a single dim glow of light from an oil lantern. The old tarp I had been covered with was pulled off of me, and I was grasped by a large burly man wearing a blue-and-green flannel shirt and some sort of blue jean overalls. I could hear him groan and grumble as he picked me up and carried me over one of his shoulders. We went down the length of the long, snow-covered driveway and then up the slippery front porch steps. He quickly hustled me through the door, which was being held open by a woman, and into a house where a fire was blazing in the fireplace. She quickly closed the door behind the big man.

The house was so much warmer than the garage where I had been hidden under that old canvas tarp for more than a week. The woman was wearing a thick red robe and fuzzy slippers, and she was hurriedly wrapping gift boxes and tying bows. Candles were lit everywhere, and their flames gave the room a very warm and inviting glow. The air was filled with the aroma of cinnamon, pumpkin, and chocolate, and there was a distinct scent of pine as well. Joyful music was quietly playing, and a mountain of ribbons, bows, tape, and wrapping paper of every design and color covered the living room floor and dining room table. I was placed out of the way and quickly dried off with a kitchen towel, as I got wet from the falling snow during the long trek from the garage to the front door of the house.

How did I get here? What is going on? I couldn't help but imagine what would happen to me and what would become of me in the future. *What kind of existence am I going to have? Who are these people and what kind of people are they?* How I ended up in the snowy shores of Lake Erie I will never know. I was scared and nervous. It was a long way from where I was from.

Suddenly, a large, excited, yellow-haired dog was

2

beside me. It circled and sniffed me, its tail wagging wildly, and it began to lick me, as I was still a little wet in some spots. It was disgusting and gross! *What is going on?* I couldn't help but wonder. With a fur-muffled thump, the dog lay down in front of me, curled up, and fell into a deep slumber. I didn't realize that dogs dreamed, barked, and apparently ran in their sleep.

I gazed down, and from certain parts of my frame, I saw a reflection that twinkled and had many different colors of lights. I gazed across into the corner of the room, and there was one of the most beautiful things imaginable. Now I knew where the pine-tree scent was coming from. Standing there was a large green pine tree covered with hundreds of brightly lit and twinkling lights, ornaments, strings of popcorn, tinsel, and decorations all around it. Underneath its boughs was a little train, slowly chugging its way around the track. It had a bright-white headlight and was puffing white smoke from the smokestack. Gift-wrapped boxes were stacked three high and four across and wrapped with some of the paper I noticed when I first was brought into the house and ribbons too. Some of the packages had candy canes and peppermint sticks tied to them with ribbon. How amazing all of this looked. On the top of the tree was an angel holding a candle. Her wings were spread far apart and wide. *Can she use those wings to fly? I wish I could fly.* I thought.

The man and woman were being very quiet, as if they were trying to hide something, for some reason keeping all of this colorful glory a secret, and I had no idea why. Only now and then would they say something to each other. *What's going on? What's the big secret on this windy, frigid, and snowy night? And why are they so quiet?*

In the warm glow of candles, twinkling lights, and the fireplace, I could make out some of the other things in the room. I saw a long wooden sled with painted-red steel runners leaning up against a wall by the tree with lights. I would share the garage with that same sled for a long, long time to come. It had a large red ribbon tied into a beautiful bow and a tag hanging off of the handle. I see a tiny toy house with little toy people in it under the tree. There were a lot of boxes and different shaped things with wrapping paper on them too. Socks hung in front of the fireplace. I counted six of them, all different sizes and colors. *Are they wet like me and hanging there to dry?*

The door leading into the room was covered with beautifully designed cards. There must have been a hundred of them on the door. It looked very nice. Above the fireplace, on the mantle, which was adorned with pine roping, were a few candles and some toy soldiers. A small plate of cookies and a tall glass of milk were sitting on the mantle as well, and nobody had touched either of them. Sticking out from under the plate was a note that was hanging slightly over the edge of the mantle so it wouldn't be overlooked. *Why is it there? Who could it be for?* My mind was racing, and I couldn't help but wonder.

In the opposite corner of the room was a big green chair with a black-and-white cat sleeping on the back of it. It didn't move when I was brought into the house.

Suddenly, without a word, the man and woman began to clean up all of the paper, tape, and ribbons. The man came over to me and moved me into the center of the room. He wiped me completely dry and checked to make sure there was not a fleck of dirt on me anywhere. He knelt down and, with one of the large rolls of paper, began to wrap me up and hide me again. He was struggling with the red, gold, and green paper and a big white bow. Twice he mumbled and tore the paper off of me and started all over again. He tried one last time, and I could see he wasn't happy with his attempt at hiding me under the paper and ribbon. He looked very tired. The woman came over to him, knelt down, took his hand, and looked into his weary eyes. Softly, she told him that a nice white bow would do just fine.

It was true. The man tied a tag with the name of Matthew to part of me. *Matthew? I wonder who Matthew is.*

The man moved me closer to the pine tree with all of the lights and ornaments and strings of popcorn and the angel on top. There was a bright flash as the man took a photograph of the tree with all of the wrapped boxes, the long red sled, the little toy house with people in it, and me. Another bright flash came as he took a photo of the fireplace mantle with the candles, empty socks, toy soldiers, glass of milk, and plate of cookies with the note. *Why is he doing this?*

The man and woman smiled and shared a tender kiss and a long hug. Suddenly, the man didn't look so grumpy and gruff. He softened, and the seriousness melted away. I could feel the love he had for this home and his family.

Without saying anything, the man and woman blew out all of the candles. The music was turned down to where I could barely hear it, and the lights on the tree were all turned off, except for the angel on the very top branch. They disappeared up the stairs, and the house became very quiet, except for the soft music. The angel's candle was the only light in the room. It was peaceful, warm, and still. The fireplace had only a faint glow of the embers. It seemed like the hours passed by slowly.

TWO

A Short, Round Man with Rosy Cheeks

I N THE NEAR DARKNESS, I began to hear the faint jingle of bells from outside of the house. Louder and louder it became but not so loud as to wake anyone. Abruptly, the jingling stopped—very close and above me. I thought I heard what sounded like footsteps, also above me. Suddenly, a heavy muffled *thumph* came from the fireplace, and I could see the ashes fly up. Instantly, a short, round man with rosy cheeks and a snow-white beard, wearing a big red suit with furry white trim, brown leather mittens, brown boots, and a red hat with a sprig of holly on it appeared from the open doors of the hearth. As he entered the room, he seemed to grow a little bit taller.

The darkened lights on the tree magically brightened and began to twinkle. It seemed he had a small, wooden, unlit pipe clenched in his teeth and was smiling at the dog, which just sat up without barking a single bark, and her tail was once again wagging wildly. He quickly tossed the big yellow dog something, and she wasted no time lying back down and began to eat it.

Slung over his right shoulder was a large pine-green velvet bag with a golden rope tie. He placed it on the floor right in front of me and pulled open the top of the bag. He began to take out many small packages that were very beautifully wrapped and stuffed all of them into the socks that were hanging by the fireplace.

Some of the things he took out of his bag weren't wrapped. I could see a harmonica, drumsticks, a small teddy bear, colored pencils, and a toy magic wand. He took out all sorts of nuts, tangerine, chocolate, and candy and placed them into the hanging socks as well. Two of the socks were stuffed more than the rest of them. He took out a dozen or more red-and-white peppermint candy canes and hung them all around the tree on its branches and a few on the pine roping along the mantle too. He scanned the tree and found a green glass ornament that looked like a pickle and proceeded to hide it deep within the tree's branches and chuckled to himself, as he was a very jolly fellow.

He then reached into the big green velvet bag and pulled out a few larger packages and placed them under the tree. He opened the small house under the tree and placed a tiny package inside of that house too. *Who is this person with all of these packages and why is he here?* I thought. He took a quick glance at me and smiled but then cocked his head with a confused look and furrowed brows.

Again, he reached into the bag quickly and pulled out something that wasn't wrapped. He attached it to me. I couldn't see what it was, but it was fastened tightly to me, and it was very shiny. He then took out a small tag and wrote a note on the tag with a quill pen that he removed from a fold in his hat, which he took off and placed on the big green chair. He attached the tag, with the note, to the object.

11

Though he was moving very quickly, he was quiet as a church mouse. Lastly, he placed a few envelopes on the tree with the names of Erika and Matthew. *Who are they? Matthew—I am beginning to understand.*

He took one last look into his bag, as it appeared to be empty now. Satisfied, he read a note left on the mantle. He chuckled again and attached a small silver bell, also taken from his hat, to one of the stockings that did not have too much stuffed into it. He then picked up the plate of cookies and the glass of milk and sat in the big green chair and put his feet on the ottoman. The cat didn't move and was still curled in a ball on the back of the chair. Licking her chops in anticipation, the dog began to drool and was looking at him. He tossed her a chunk of one of the cookies. He seemed to be in no hurry now.

After taking the unlit pipe out of his mouth and putting it in his coat pocket, he dipped the cookies, one by one, into the milk and ate them—savoring every bite. He enjoyed all six of them and finished the milk without getting one drop on his big white beard.

He placed his red-and-white furry hat back atop his balding, silver-haired head. He stood and placed the empty plate and glass neatly together on the mantle and jotted a short note on the napkin and chuckled again. Next, he put his fur-lined, brown leather mittens on. He then gathered up his empty green velvet bag, patted the cat on its head, and leaned over and hugged the dog. Entering the fireplace from where he came, he took one long, final look at the tree, nodded his approval, and touched the side of his nose. And with a wink of his left eye he disappeared.

I could hear the bells jingle again, but the sound faded away quickly into the night. The music stopped then, and the tree's lights dimmed to dark by themselves; even the angel's candle was now dark. The embers in the fireplace eventually went cold. All was quiet and still. The ticking clock on the mantle was the only sound to be heard. The dog went upstairs too. It had been an exciting and interesting beginning for me.

THREE

I Can't Believe It!

MORNING CAME AFTER WHAT SEEMED like a long, still, and quiet night. I heard movement above me and the sound of people I did not hear the night before. Little people noises, they were. In the distance I could hear church bells ringing. Six chimes rang out. There was a flurry of movement on the floors above me. I heard many little footsteps moving back and forth across the length of the house. Then I could hear the thuds of larger footsteps and a warning to wait until they were called down.

I heard the larger footsteps coming down the stairs. It was the man again. He was wearing slippers and an old checkered, blue flannel robe, with a red, long-sleeved shirt and flannel pajamas beneath the robe. His hair was off to one side, as if he hadn't moved at all while he was asleep. I heard him mumble something about it being only six o'clock and wishing it were seven. But diligently he began to perform his tasks. Candles were lit, the tree lights were turned on, and holiday music once again permeated the air. He sat in the chair, his camera resting on his crossed legs at the ready.

The woman from the night before entered the room, too, with two cups of something that was steaming hot. The man smiled and thanked her as she handed him one of the steaming cups.

The okay was given for the noisemakers who were still upstairs to come down. In a flash, there came what seemed to be a stampede of footsteps on the stairs. *How many people can there be up there?* I wondered.

I was shocked to see only two little people and the big yellow dog come flying around the corner into the big room with the tree. Almost breathless, the two children were wide-eyed with amazement. It hit me then why the man and woman had been so quiet and secretive last evening.

The ten-year-old girl, Erika, saw the dollhouse under the tree and crossed her hands on her chest as if she were speechless and silently giving thanks, falling to both of her knees in front of it. The little boy saw the sled first and put his hands on his cheeks as if he were shocked.

He turned toward the tree, saw me, and rushed toward me, screaming, "I can't believe it! I can't believe it!

"It's for me!?" he half exclaimed and half asked. He quickly checked the tag and knew for sure I was his gift.

Now I knew for certain who Matthew was. He tore the big white bow away from me and pulled me away from all of the other gifts and the tree. I could feel the excitement in the eight-year-old's hands as he grabbed me and straightened me until I was upright. He would turn nine before he rode me for the first time. He was practically shaking with joy. He said, "It's almost too big for me!"

The man, his father, told him that he would be just fine, as he would grow into it quickly.

Matthew exclaimed, "It's beautiful! I can't believe I finally have my own big two-wheeled bicycle. And it's my favorite color, green, too! Look here; it says it was made in Chicago."

He grasped the thing the man in the red suit had attached to my handlebars and read the note on the tag aloud. It was from Santa Claus, and it read, "I hope you enjoy this on your new bike that your mother and father gave you for Christmas." He gave the thing a big squeeze.

A loud *honk* came out of it, and the dog began to bark and the cat bolted off the back of the chair and ran down the hall, while Matthew's father nearly spilled his steaming-hot drink.

As it would turn out, Santa Claus would put a new accessory for me in Matthew's stocking for the next several years.

Matthew then put my kickstand back down and ran over to his parents. Joined by Erika, they enjoyed a big family group hug and bowed their heads. The father thanked someone for being born on this day, and then the family wished each other an honest and loving merry Christmas.

Quickly, the kids were back to the tree. They took turns and quietly read aloud the cards that were placed on the Christmas tree. They carefully pulled their stockings away from the mantle, dumped them out onto the floor, and opened all of the neatly wrapped little packages that Santa had placed inside. Eating chocolates and treats from their stockings, they opened the rest of the gifts from the under the tree and passed out gifts to their parents. Their mother smiled adoringly as the children went about the business of opening and passing out the rest of the gifts.

All the meanwhile, there were flashes from the camera, and nobody seemed to notice. Matthew kept his eye on me in between opening his other gifts.

Erika soon curled up on the sofa next to her mother after opening all of her gifts and was already reading one of her new books.

Then it came to me. The sun had come up, and it was very sunny and bright outside. And I realized something. I wasn't scared and nervous anymore. I felt I was going to have an awesome existence with these nice people and my boy, Matthew.

FOUR

Maiden Ride

FOR A FEW WEEKS AFTER Christmas, I was able to stay in the warm, dry house. Then, when the decorations were taken down and the furniture was rearranged, I had to go back to the garage and was parked next to Erika's red two-wheeler she had gotten the Christmas before. Her bike had different colored streamers coming from the handlebars and a white basket on the front that had daisies attached to it. She had a long, curved center bar instead of the straight bar a boy's bike had. Attached to her handlebars was a bell she could ring, but she never did. Underneath the back of her seat was a license plate that was red, too, with her name, in raised letters, stamped on it. Erika kept her bike very neat with no scratches, dents, or dirt. I hoped that trait ran in the family.

I didn't mind the waiting in the garage because Erika bike was nice, and I knew what spring was bringing. It was a long winter. The big sled with the painted red runners got a lot of action that first winter. The deep Lake Erie shoreline snow didn't melt until near the end of March, and the April rains kept me in the garage a couple of weeks longer.

Then that warm sunny day came when everything was dry and the sun was out. Matthew and his dad came into the garage and checked the pressure in both of my tires and walked me to the end of the long driveway. As they walked, his father told him to take it slow and easy until he was comfortable and confident in turning and stopping. His dad lowered the seat as low as it would go and the handlebars as well to match my now nine-year-old's size. Matthew pushed my left pedal halfway forward and slung his right leg over my seat. His right foot was nowhere near the pedal. He pushed off with his left foot on the left pedal, and we were on our way.

For the very first time, I was being ridden. Matthew's feet nearly left the pedals as each pedal rounded to the bottom of the rotation. It seemed forever since I'd been made in Chicago the previous November. My boy's hands were a little shaky at first, and a couple of times I thought we would ride off of the sidewalk, and I imagined us going into the yard of every house we passed as my front tire veered left and then right and left again.

Matthew quickly got better. By the end of the block, he glided to a smooth stop without making my back tire skid on the smooth, gray flagstone sidewalk. He wasn't permitted to ride on the street just yet. He had to get off of me to turn around. In doing that, he nearly had to let me fall over before he could get off. He held on tightly to me, though, and didn't let me hit the ground. But it was close.

Many of Matthew's friends lived on the same block. They were all around the same age and either in third or fourth grade at Harrison Elementary School. Some of the names I recall are Jimmy, Johnny, Nate, Bobby, and Hank. A lot of them came out of their homes as we rode by just to see my boy riding his favorite Christmas gift. How could they not? He was yelling with excitement as we passed each house.

Matthew's friends had been hearing about me for over three months now and wanted to see if I lived up to his descriptions. The return trip back up the block didn't go as quickly as the first trip down to the corner had. He had to stop at each boy's house and let his friend look me over.

All of them were in awe and, I could tell, envious as well. They liked the sparkling, radiant-green color with white trim on my fenders and chain guard. Each kid had to take a turn at honking my incredibly loud horn. When neighborhood dogs started barking, they only honked it more. Matthew's somewhat anxious father, who was still waiting on the steps of their front porch, could hear the horn honking and knew that everything was okay.

The boys all wanted to take me for a spin, but he told them his dad said nobody was allowed to ride it but him. I can tell you, that wouldn't last for very long that summer.

When he finally arrived back at his house, his dad, who had gone back in the house, came outside and asked how it had gone.

"It went just swell!" replied a very proud and happy boy.

Now it was his dad's turn, as he just had to take me for a trip around the block. What a difference to have this big, husky man riding on me. I could feel the power in his legs, and when he would stand up to pedal up the hill, my sprocket creaked as I swayed side to side with each downward push. And my pedals could feel the pressure of his work boots as I powered forward. My chain tightened, each tooth on the sprocket latching onto the chain links as it went around and around. What a difference that was from Matthew's black high-top tennis shoes.

I wouldn't feel that sort of power again for many years. Yeah, my boy did grow up with me, but he never reached the size of his father, or at least his weight.

When we made the turn to come down the block to our house, the weight of the father's boot pressed heavy on my coaster breaks. Without trying, he left a pretty long skid Matthew on the sidewalk right in front of his house. He didn't really mean to do that and told my boy to avoid doing that as much as possible.

That is kind of funny now that I think about it. Many of my tires needed to be replaced because of that same thing. Why is it so cool to see who can make the longest skid Matthew? I never got that!

FIVE

Meet the Gang

SOON AFTER THE MAIDEN RIDE down our block, Matthew and I started to meet up daily with every one of his friends that had a bike. Believe it or not, not everyone had a bike. So the boys that did have a bike were actually very lucky. Every day after school, my boy would come home, do his homework, and eat dinner. And then (if he hadn't any chores to do) he'd call one of his buddies.

Soon, we'd be flying down the block, wind whistling through my spokes and my horn honking, on our way to another one of his friend's house. From there, the two of them would go to another buddy's house, where two more of his friends would be. And then the four would go to another house, where two more of his friends would be, and so on.

Then sometimes, as a big gang, we'd all head across town to the basketball courts, and the boys would play basketball. Being that it was still early spring, it seemed to be thing to do. Every time was the same. The boys would play basketball for a little while and then end up on the benches near where we bikes were parked, and they would start talking about the bikes.

Do boys talk about anything else? Not when they are nine and ten years old. Well, maybe they talked a little more about baseball.

I was a big topic of the conversation that first year, as I was the shiny newcomer. My rims were gleaming. The big round white walled tires made me look bigger than I really was. I didn't always have those kind of tires, as mine would need replaced many times over the year. My handlebars were as shiny as can be, with no scratches, and sun reflected off them brilliantly. My horn was chrome with a big black rubber ball that, when squeezed, made an amazingly loud honk. I was the one every one of his friends wanted to have or at least take for a ride. The other bikes in the gang had their own stories of glory and their own issues as well.

Jimmy's bike was a bright red with white fenders and all-black tires. Instead of a horn, a bell was attached to the handlebars. His bike had a slightly bent back rim that made it wobble a bit when going above a certain speed. That little wobble would never slow Jimmy down though. Jimmy had received his bike last year for his birthday, so his bike was over a year older than me but very nice still, even with a few scratches. It was very shiny and clean but had that bent rear rim Jimmy's father refused to fix for a third time. I guess that's why my boy's father told Matthew to never go over big curbs with me.

Attached to the rear and underneath Jimmy's bike's seat was a leather pouch that held all sorts of things. Jimmy would always have his Cub Scout pocketknife with him, plus a couple of wrenches and an extra baseball, and it was always stuffed with what seemed like a hundred pieces of bubblegum. Jimmy was always chewing bubblegum and could blow a bubble inside a bubble. He could blow two bubbles at the same time out of both sides of his mouth too. The boy had talent.

He shared his stash of gum with all the boys. Jimmy had a generous soul. I found out later that Jimmy's older sister worked at the candy counter at the big department store in town and would bring home bubblegum for Jimmy if he would wash the dishes when it was her turn. By the way, Jimmy was my boy's best friend.

Johnny's bike was fire-engine red with white pin stripes. His bike had a rack over the back fender with an old leather belt wound between the basket's frame. Johnny strapped his jacket to it when it got too warm to wear it. Johnny's bike had handlebars that were so scratched up they didn't shine anymore. Both handgrips had the handlebars poking through them. That was because he rarely used his kickstand and just threw his bike to the ground when he stopped and got off. That bike sure took a beating. It was scratched everywhere and not taken care of at all. The chain hadn't been oiled since it was new. Johnny's bike had cracked reflectors, dented fenders, and one of the pedals was missing one of the rubber tread pieces. The front fender was dented so badly it rubbed on the tire and made a howling noise when Johnny rode. It sounded like his bike was in pain. Johnny looked at me with an envious eye, and I shuddered to think what would happen if he ever got his hands on me.

Then there was Bobby's bike. Bobby wasn't the first boy to own his bike and maybe not the second either. It was old—probably from the early 1940s. It was green like me but not a radiant green. It was a dark green, with tires that weren't as wide as the rest of ours. It had no stripes or stickers, with only one red reflector attached to the back fender. Under the seat post on the frame was a tag that said, "GI." None of us knew what that meant. When the pedals turned, there was a pretty loud creak or squeak—I couldn't tell which—or maybe both. The manufacturer's tag had an *H* stamped on it. The handlebars and rims were not chrome like the rest of us but were painted. That bike didn't have a chain guard, so Bobby had to put his right pants leg in his sock or put a rubber band around his pants as not to get it caught in the chain. Bobby was told his bike was made completely of steel and had no copper or nickel metal in it. He said he heard his father call his bicycle a "Victory bicycle." Nobody knew what that meant, but it sure sounded important.

Bobby's bike had a double basket mounted on the back that drapes over both sides of the back tire. Bobby was a paper boy and that was where he put the newspapers when he had to do his route every morning before school. Apparently, that bike was also a working bike. It was no wonder it looked so worn and tired all of the time. But that bike still could keep up with us when we were zooming around town. It was always well oiled, had new tires, and seemed to never ever break down. We all looked up to it for some reason. I think we all secretly wished to be around as long as this bike had been around, especially Johnny's bike.

Bobby did take good care of him too. Bobby's older brother taught him how to oil the chain, tighten the nuts and bolts, and keep the air in the tires inflated and how to change a tire when there was a flat. Bobby would help all the boys do some sort of work on all of us over the next several years.

Hank's bike was really cool. First of all, it was the only one of us that had a metal flake paint job. He was a really bright, metallic silver and blue. But that wasn't what made this bike cool. It was a three-speed, and Hank could beat all of us up any hill in our town. Racing Hank was, at best, a second-place finish if he used his different gears. The metallic and silver looked fast just standing still and leaning on it's kickstand. There were other cool things on it as well. Between the spokes, there were reflectors that were yellow and red discs. The rest of us only had one red reflector on our back fenders. Reflectors helped us to be seen at nighttime by car headlights. These reflectors were arranged so that, when the wheels were spinning, they looked like spirals turning. It also had hand brakes too, with really bright-white cables that ran down the length of the bike and attached to the frame by the back tire. There was one for the front wheel as well. Nobody else in the group had hand brakes.

Hank's bike had mirrors with chrome frames and posts on both handle bars, too, and a bell instead of a horn. That made his bike look bigger than the rest of us, but it wasn't really. This bike had so much chrome it probably didn't need even a single reflector. It also had a light that was mounted as close to the center of the handlebars as possible. Like both fenders, it was shiny chrome and was operated by batteries and shined pretty far at night. I only know this because, every now and then, Hank would ride over to our house at night. Matthew wasn't allowed to ride me too much after dark because I didn't have a light mounted on me—at least not this first year. When the streetlights came on, we had to be heading on our way home.

Here is the one thing that Hank's bike had that made him seem very cool. He had a rack that was attached above his front fender. There was a two-toned blue-and-white seat with bright-white handgrips. The silver metallic and blue was streamlined and sleek and had been made at the same place I was made in Chicago. It was a tall two-wheeler like me, so that sort of made us cousins. I was newer and little bit shinier, but Hank's bike had a lot of extras that really made it special. Hank took good care of it too, like I hoped Matthew would take care of me. Maybe someday I would get some neat accessories like Hank's bike has, maybe just a few. I did have the biggest and loudest horn though.

Finally there was Nate's bike. This bike was known as "good ol'" Nate's bike. He wasn't abused like Johnny's bike, but it was continuously being embarrassed by Nate. Nate's family didn't have enough money to add accessories like Hank's did to his bike, but Nate still wanted to have "stuff" on his bike. So he would find certain things and attach them to it, or he would use old things that were given to him. For instance, there was the headlight issue. Nate's parents would not go out of the way to buy Nate anything to put on his bike, and for some reason, it was never on his Christmas list either. I would hear them say he was lucky just to have a bike.

So Nate would improvise. For a headlight, Nate used black electrical tape and taped an old dented metal flashlight, which he'd found in a ditch, to the front left fork of his bike. It looked ridiculous, but Nate was allowed to ride at night because of it. He was always re-taping it, as the electrical tape didn't hold too well. For a basket, Nate took an old metal milk bottle crate and wired it to the front of the handlebars. It worked great, and all of the boys would throw their baseball gloves, balls, and jackets in there. It just looked ridiculous hanging in front of that bike, but Nate didn't seem to care. He thought it was pretty cool. Nobody ever said anything to Nate about the way he would rig things to his bike. Everything he tried worked. He and Hank became best friends.

That was the gang. Other kids would move to our block and then move away, but this group would grow up together and be friends for as long as I could remember. Like some of the kids, some of us bikes would come and go over the years as well. But for now, this group was close, and we would be a big part of the boy's lives and share in some pretty important parts of their growing up. I know I was a big part of my boy's life.

My First Summer

THERE ARE SOME THINGS THAT burn a memory into your mind like no other things. For me, it is certain sounds. One of those sounds was the one that my tires would make when riding around a corner where there was a little bit of gravel or grit on the road. It had to be dry for a few days, and we had to be going a certain speed and take the corner just right so the outside wall of my tire hit the gravel perfectly to make that noise. To me, that's one of the sounds that defined summer.

Our streets were paved, but we had hard winters. When it snowed or was icy, the city plow trucks would put rock salt or sand or both on the roads so cars wouldn't slide around bends and end up in a ditch off the road or slide through stop signs and wreck into other cars. So there was always some sort of gravel on the roads in our town. The street sweepers did a great job picking up a lot of it, but they couldn't get it all and would leave just enough for my tires to make that sound. The sound of grinding sand or little stones into the pavement when my tire would turn through it is so comforting. I love it.

Sometimes my tread would pick up a little pebble and it would get stuck in between the grooved rubber treads of my tire. Sometimes when we were riding at high speeds, the pebble would come loose and slam into the underneath side of one of my fenders and make a loud *tink* sound. Neither Matthew nor I would know when that was about to happen, and it always startled both of us.

My first summer was full of discovery for my boy and me, his bike. Even though I am so old now, if I had the chance one more time to roll down our block and hear the gravel grind underneath my tires, I would be instantly transported back to that first summer. It was a season of discovery, and sounds were a big part of that.

Some of the other sounds that bring me right back to those days when I was in my prime are so distinctive. There was the distinctive creaking of the garage door swinging open. It made a different noise in the summer than it did in the winter. Why is that? There was the sound a whistle with the little ball in it makes—the kind the lifeguards, coaches, crossing guards, and traffic cops use. That sound, it seemed, always signaled something important. When we were at the pool and I was locked to the fence, I would first hear that whistle, and then somebody was getting in trouble for something. At the ball fields, I would hear that whistle, and then a man would bark some instructions at the boys and, still to this day, I have no idea what about. I never heard the boys complain about the yelling. When school was in, and we would ride to school instead of walk, we would always hear the crossing guard blow her whistle just as we whizzed past her. For years, I thought we were doing the right thing and that was her way of saying hello or good morning. I couldn't have been more wrong. I guess that's why it's called a cross*walk* and not a cross *ride*!

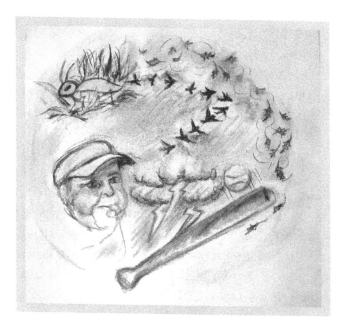

Another sound I can recall is the crack of a baseball bat hitting a ball at the ball fields. There was nothing quite like the sound of a rawhide-covered baseball being struck by a solid wood baseball bat made from a white ash tree from the northeastern forest in Pennsylvania and upstate New York. Bats also had very cool nicknames, like Lumber, Timber, Crusher, The Stick, and Long Ball Smasher. The ball also made another sound as it was caught in a perfectly oiled and broken-in mitt. The mitts were made out of cowhide, or rawhide as it was called.

My boy's mitt was made by a very well know mitt maker. His was the gold glove, all-star's edition glove that was handed down to him from his older cousin. It wasn't new, but it was the perfect glove for my boy. It almost made a popping noise when it was caught just right. I would hear that sound a thousand times a summer for many years, when my boy would play catch with his dad in the front yard. I would be parked on the sidewalk. I absolutely love that sound. To me, it sounds like the love between a boy and his father. They would do that for hours and hours and would talk about anything and everything.

Crickets in late summer had a sound that defined the season. If any bug could define a season, the cricket was the champion of that. The chirping seemed to go faster when the air was warmer and slower when it was not so warm. The rain falling on our flat garage roof was a soothing sound. It meant I would get to rest for a while. It would start slowly where you could hear the individual pitter-patter of raindrops until they were so numerous it sounded like one constant roar. Sometimes the rain was accompanied by a low rolling thunder far off in the distance, and sometimes the thunder was so loud we thought the garage was going to fall in on top of us.

Another sound I remember well is the sound of the hose water when Matthew was washing me. The sound of the jet stream of water on my wide metal fenders made a metallic metal humming sound. It tickled a little bit, and it was the sound of me getting clean and shiny.

Those glorious sounds of the summer season are unlike the sounds of any other season. The only sounds I recall from autumn were the rustle of leaves blowing in the wind and the Canadian geese honking as they migrated south for the winter across Lake Erie. The crunch of the leaves would muffle the sounds of my tires on the gravel. In winter, the sound I recall most was the howling wind, with sleet and snow hitting the garage windows. There was also the sound of snow shovels scraping along the asphalt driveway and the flagstone sidewalks. That meant the snow was deep.

In spring, the main sound I remember was the return of the songbirds early in the morning—a beautiful sound that would echo through the neighborhood long before the sun would rise. The other sound of spring I can recall was the sound of the frogs, the spring peepers, along the paths we would ride in the woods. Of all of the seasons and all of the sounds, though, I truly miss the sounds of summer. It always seemed like our summertime would race by in a flash. That first year certainly did.

SEVEN

Let's Race!

I T WAS MY SECOND SUMMER now, and the boys were a year older and had grown about two to three inches in height. All of them were stronger now and could handle us bikes very well with a year of experience under their belts. It sure felt good to be out and on the road. Yes, on the road finally! This past Christmas, I'd had a brand-new generator light put on me by Santa Claus. It was imported from England I had heard his father saying. I had to be moving for the light to work, but it shone bright, and I had a red taillight as well. With that light, we were now allowed to ride at night but just around our street and one block over. That was just perfect too, because one block over would soon become very important for the boys.

If there is one thing you can be sure of, it is this. Boys love to race their bikes. Boys just like to race period. It could be a footrace around the house, a three-legged race at camp, a swimming race across the pool, a race up the steps at school, or a race of bullfrogs caught at the pond. They would race earthworms after a hard rain, race to see who could eat a hot dog the fastest, or race to see who could chew a piece of bubblegum and blow a bubble first (Jimmy was almost always the winner). You name it, and it can become a race. It starts when the boys have their first tricycles, and by the time they get to have full-size bikes like me, they are quite the serious racers.

A lot of things go into becoming a good racer. First, you have to have a bike that can take high speeds without any vibrations, and the chain needs to stay on the sprockets too. Secondly, you have to have your tires inflated with the right amount of air, and the tire tread has to be in good shape to hold the road on the turns. Finally, the most important thing, you have to have a boy who's strong enough and who won't chicken out when it gets close and doesn't hesitate on the turns. That's when accidents happen. Let me tell you, the accidents did happen.

When the boys were bored and sitting around with nothing better to do, somebody would utter those words that most of us just loved to hear. "Let's have a race!" Some of the boys got too nervous and didn't want to do it and, at that time, could suddenly hear their mothers calling them from across the neighborhood. Others were nervous because their bikes just weren't up to the challenge.

And there were those of us bikes that got as excited as the boys. It was like we were meant to do it from the time we are built. Why have racing stripes painted on us if we weren't meant to race?

On our block, we had major rules that had to be followed. If anyone got caught cheating, it was an instant disqualification. The rules were simple and as follows: No more than three of us could race at the same time. No cutting the corners or through yards. No interference with other racers. The most important rule, if someone crashed, the race was over no matter who was in the lead or how close to the finish.

Usually it was just the six of us, and we would race one of two ways. We would have races with just two of us at a time, or we would have a race with three of us at a time. It was a really creative process, and it always seemed to be fair.

There was one particular race I can recall in detail. There were six of us, and the boys decided to race in pairs. The winners of the preliminary heats would race a three-bike race for the block championship of that particular week or until the next race.

How the boys decided to race each other was really cool. Sometimes they would use a baseball bat and do the hand-over-hand method. They would start with their hands on the thick barrel end of the bat and start moving their hands over each other's hands toward the skinny bottom handle of the bat. The last hand that ended up covered that end of the bat handle would be one of the ones to race. Another method was for each boy to put one of his shoes with toes pointed into the center of a circle and recite a strange limerick called, "Bubblegum Bubble Gum in a Dish":

One kid would recite the poem and point to a different shoe on each word of the poem. When it ended, whoever's shoe his finger was on was one of the kids who had to wait. The last two kids in the circle would race. Weird I know, but it worked great.

The whole limerick went like this:

Bubblegum, bubblegum in a dish.
How many pieces do you wish?
[Pick a number] Seven.
One, two, three, four, five, six, seven.
You are not the one to be picked.

Whosever shoe was pointed on when the word *picked* was said had to wait. The whole process would be done until there were two kids left, and they would be the ones to race first. Then the process would be done again for the other four and so on. This process went on for more than just bike races. It was done for choosing up sides for baseball games, marbles, or anything that needed a fair way of making a choice about something or who was going to be "it" or picked.

There were other limericks they used, too, for choosing who was picked. My favorite was one called, "Engine, Engine Number 9." It went:

> Engine, engine number 9,
> Going down Chicago line.
> If the train should jump the track,
> Do you want your money back?
> [pick yes or no]
> Y-E-S spells yes, and you are the one
> to be picked.

Can you guess why this one was my favorite?

After the sides were chosen, the boys decided who was going first by doing it by alphabetical order.

Did I ever mention these boys were pretty sharp?

45

The Race

BOBBY AND JIMMY WERE TO go first. The course was simple and not too long, but there was a hill. And hills always made the race more interesting. They started at the top of the street and came down the hill and picked up speed all the way to the stop sign at the bottom of the hill. From there, they had to make a sharp left turn and zoom over to the next block, race along the flat and then up the hill to another stop sign and back over to our block, where they'd started from. Once at the top of our hill, they had to race down our hill to our driveway and, of course, skid to a stop. Whosever front wheel crossed the middle of our driveway first was the winner.

It took just over three minutes to race around the block. If it took much longer, we knew there was a problem on the other block. And we knew what that problem usually was, and it wasn't good.

Finally, the two rounded the corner at the top

of the street, and it looked like an even race. Down the hill they came, both pedaling as fast as they could. Their hair was pasted straight back because of the wind. Wait, hair? What happened to their ball caps? They must have blown off during the race. They crossed our driveway in a dead tie, and both began to skid to a stop. Jimmy stopped just before Bobby, so he was determined the winner. That was one of the closest two bike races ever on our block, and it was still talked about by some of the boys during their college years. Ties at the finish line were determined by who came to a skidding stop first.

Matthew and I raced Nate and his classic/vintage 1940s bike. Even with all of the stuff hanging off of it, Nate and his bike gave us a really good race. We grabbed the lead early, but they were nipping at my back fender the whole rest of the way. Even when we skidded to a stop in front of our house, Nate bumped into my back wheel, and Matthew nearly lost control of me. No damage was done, but it startled me, as that was the first time I had been close to crashing.

Hank and the metallic silver-and-blue three-speed had to race Johnny and his red collection of scrapes, scratches, dents, and rust. Hank wasn't happy about having to race Johnny. If Johnny didn't care about his own bike, why would he care about any of the other bikes? We were always afraid he would run into us just to knock us down so we would get some scratches and dents on us too. Or maybe we would get some spokes knocked out and our rims twisted out of line. It was just spooky. Johnny had a fierce look in his eye when he would race. The other boys always thought he was just trying to make us think he was crazy, and maybe someone would let him win a race on purpose. Maybe Johnny was misguided for thinking that, as nobody ever let anyone win on purpose—not in this neighborhood. Winning a race was a big deal, and the bragging didn't stop until the next race. And then sometimes it just didn't stop ever.

Their race started out just fine, but halfway into the first turn, Johnny's front wheel was so close to Hank's back wheel that it actually rubbed tires and made an ominous vibrating noise. Hank almost lost control and barked at Johnny for almost making him crash. It should have been an instant disqualification, but they raced on. The rest of the race was neck and neck.

Yes, it's true that Hank had a three-speed, but for "official" races, Hank had to keep his bike in the second gear, which was similar to all of the other single-speed bikes in the race. This made it fair, and the race would be won or lost on the skill and strength of the boy. Hank and Johnny were about the same size and body structure. In a footrace Johnny was always the fastest. But Hank didn't like to lose and was very competitive in everything he did—sports, school, board games. And later on, even with girls, Hank was always trying to be number one.

You could hear them yelling at each other on the other block and could tell that both racers were taking risks to win this race. We knew this because you could hear car horns blowing. That meant they were not paying close attention to traffic. Traffic could determine the winner, but that was part of racing around the block, and everyone was okay with that. It could become very dangerous.

As they rounded the corner at the top of our street, Hank and the tall silver and blue had about a bicycle's length lead on Johnny and the red twenty-six-inch with the scratches, dents, and dry rusty chain. Johnny quickly gained on Hank as they came down the hill. It looked like it was going to be another skid to the finish. This was where Hank had the advantage of stopping. His bike had both front and back hand brakes, as well as coaster pedal brakes and could come to a stop faster than the rest of us with just the rear coaster brake. We could make longer skids though.

They crossed the finish line and it was hard to tell who was first even though it looked like Hank had Johnny by about half a wheel's length. They both skidded to a stop, and Hank had beaten Johnny in that he was able to skid to a stop in half of the distance. Johnny was so upset he argued about the fairness and accused Hank of shifting gears on the hill, and Hank accused Johnny of nearly crashing into him on the turns.

The rest of us decided that Hank was the winner due to the quick skidding stop, and the argument was over. Those were the rules, and Johnny knew it. It was proposed that, for future races after this day, Hank had to use only his coaster brakes.

I think that these races sometimes defined the character of the boys. It could bring out a certain intensity not seen when they were doing anything else. It must have been very important to all of them.

NINE

The Finish

AFTER THE FIRST THREE RACES, it was time for the final. Hank's metallic silver-and-blue bike, Jimmy's red and white bike with the bent rim and I were the winners of our races. It was nearly an unfair race, as the silver and blue did have a few advantages the rest of us didn't have. He did have the three speeds, even if he had to keep it in second gear. He had the dual braking system too. All of the boys tried to tell Hank he could only use one brake, but he swore the rear brake on his bike was not as good as ours, and he had to use two to stop quickly. They agreed just to be safe but just for today's race.

We lined up. Hank was next to the curb on his left, Jimmy was in the middle, and I was all the way on the outside, which made it tougher to handle the wide left turns if we were close together—especially in the spring or early summer when there was still a lot of winter sand and gravel on the roads. Another nerve-racking thing the boys never took into consideration was the fact that all of us bikes were almost too big for these boys. Even though the boys had grown, we bikes were still big, especially for this second summer. We all had twenty-six-inch wheels and medium-to-large frames. None of the boys were very tall or strong yet. Being able to handle us with the nimble agility of a teenager wouldn't come until the following summer or perhaps even the next after that. We were all afraid of crashing and getting all bent up or broken, but the boys wanted to race nevertheless.

It was time to start. Nate was the official who started us, and all of the boys would be the officials to see how the race ended. They discussed it and decided that Bobby would follow the racers just to make sure everything was done fair and square. After the argument that Hank and Johnny had about their race, the boys only thought that to be the fairest way of doing it. Nate lined the boys up and told them to get ready. The front of each tire was lined up even with the edge of the driveway at the top of the hill.

Nate raised both arms with his hands above his head. He shouted, *"On your marks!"*

The boys' hearts were already racing, and their sweaty palms gripped the hard rubber handgrips.

"Get ready!"

The boys adjusted their high-top tennis shoes on the rubber pads of the pedals.

On "Go!!" he quickly dropped both of his hands together and motioned toward the bottom of the street. We were off

It seemed like it had taken a full minute for him to say go ...

Hank and Jimmy got the jump on Matthew and me, and by the first turn, we were the full length of a bicycle behind them. That was okay because now we didn't have to venture out wide into the sand and gravel, where it was almost certain we would have slipped and crashed. Or at the least, we would have fallen even farther behind.

As we rounded the second turn, it was Hank and the metallic silver and blue, Jimmy and the red and white bike with the bent rim, and Matthew riding me, the newer radiant green. My boy was pumping my pedals as fast as he could. I could feel the power, and he was really making us go fast—the fastest ever.

We made up some distance and pulled to the outside of Jimmy, and when we rounded the second turn, we were even with him. Then came the long hill, and that was always a test for the boys. All the boys were breathing heavy and pedaling as fast as they could go. The red and I were gaining quickly on the silver and blue. Hank always shifted into an easier gear when riding, so he hadn't built up the leg strength the other boys with single-speed bikes had. By the time we got to the top of the hill, we were as even as when we'd started the race. Finally, the final turn was upon us. I was on the outside, so I would lose a little ground as we made the turn.

One hundred downhill yards to go from the turn to our driveway, Jimmy and Hank were still even. And the final turn to go down our street came quickly. Luckily, there was no traffic this time, and we were able to share the entire road. As we went into the last turn, Hank, who was still on the curb lane, drifted out just a little. It was by accident, as we were going very fast at this point and not slowing down to take the turn. Jimmy didn't yield an inch of his position, and the two boys nearly tangled pedals and began to wobble wildly. It seemed as if they were going to lose control and crash. Only for an instant, for one rotation of the pedals, they had to stop pedaling to avoid contact and instant disqualification. Also, a crash here would have been disastrous, as it was in an intersection, and traffic could be heavy at times. They had to stop pedaling to avoid the disaster. They stopped pedaling!

This was our chance, as we were way on the outside of both of them and not tangled up with them. Matthew kept pedaling and took a quick look at the both of them just to be sure he wouldn't get caught and crashed into. Way out along the outside of the turn, where the gravel and sand was, he pedaled through it. We seemed to pass the others easily and had a slim lead as the street's hill caused all of the racers to gain amazing speed.

Halfway down the hill, Hank and Jimmy had recovered and were right on our tail. We could see the finish line, and the boys at the driveway were crouching, waiting and watching us with great anticipation. They knew it was a good race, and whoever won this one would have truly earned it. Fifty yards to go, and you could hear the hum of the silver and blue's tires and creak of Jimmy's rear sprocket. Wind was whistling through my spokes like never before. They were very close and gaining with every downhill yard we covered. Matthew was pumping as hard as he could, but I could tell he was getting tired. Still, he had no quit in him, as he hated to lose as much as Hank liked to win. He wasn't like Hank, who always needed to win. But my boy, a fierce competitor in his own right, did not like losing.

We were still ahead as the finish line was rapidly drawing closer. Twenty-five yards now, and in a few brief seconds, it would be over. I could feel Hank and Jimmy as they closed in on us. Their front wheels were now even with the back of my front fender and gaining with every pump of their pedals, but we were pumping too. Now to the finish line to see who would win this amazing race—one of the closest three bike races in the history of Charles Avenue.

Just as our front wheel crossed the line by our driveway, Matthew slammed his right foot down hard on my pedal, and my back wheel locked up and we began to skid. When we came to a stop, my back tire felt very warm, and I think there was a little gray smoke from the skid that was over twelve feet long. Hank and Jimmy were skidding as well, and we thought we had lost because Hank was able to come to a stop before both of us. The boys waiting at the finish line called the winner. Hank pumped both fists in the air, as he knew he was the winner again.

But this time, he was wrong, and that was not the case—not the case at all! The boys rushed over to Matthew and me, his radiant-green two-wheeler, and mobbed him. Patting him on the back, they congratulated us as the winners by almost half a wheel! They were even more impressed by the super long skid Matthew made at the end of the race.

"What a race! What a race!" the boys kept exclaiming. They went on and on with the congratulatory comments and talking about how amazing it was to watch from the bottom of the hill that last hundred or so yards. Matthew was so happy and excited, like all winners are. But this was special, as it was his first big race win on his tall, radiant-green boy's two-wheeler bike.

Then the boys went over to Jimmy and his tall red bike and claimed them as the second-place finishers. Jimmy's eyes showed complete surprise, and he acted as if he'd actually had won the race. This was one of the only times of all the races ever done around our block where the second-place finisher was so happy. Jimmy had beaten Hank by only a few inches.

Matthew and Jimmy would become best friends and remained so as far I can tell. Hank was distraught and couldn't believe it. He nearly threw a tantrum like many boys his age tend to do when they lose a race or any contest. His beautiful silver-and-blue three-speed with the shock absorber front forks, mirrors, a bell, a cool battery-operated headlight, and dual hand brakes had come in third place just inches behind the front tire of Jimmy's bright-red single-speed with white fenders and all-black tires, not to mention the slightly bent back rim. It was clear that looks and accessories didn't make you a winner—a lesson the boys would learn over and over again as they grew up.

The boys, except for Johnny, didn't seem to notice how upset Hank was about losing. He quietly grinned at the whole affair but never uttered a word to anyone.

TEN

Girls

Not long after the big race, the boys noticed there was a group of girls about the same age as them who always seemed to be riding by and looking at them strangely. Yes, they had bikes too. At first, the girls would ride past the boys and just look at them and quickly look away and giggle. What? The boys didn't do anything funny.

Then the girls started riding by and waving, before coming back the other way and waving again.

Then one time, one of the girls, in that high-pitched young girl voice and drawing her words out way long, said as they rode past, "Hi, Matthew."

At this age, boys really didn't want anything to do with girls, except for the fact that they had some cool bikes too—for girl's bikes anyway. Caught by surprise and not lacking manners, Matthew said, "Hello," back and waved as they went by.

The boys looked at my boy and really gave him

the business like never before. They slugged him in the arm, yanked his tucked-in shirt out, gave him wet willies, knocked off his baseball cap, and messed up his hair. What was he thinking saying hello to a girl he didn't even know? Didn't he know that he was about to start something? Something not one of these boys wanted to start? Not just yet anyway.

These girls seemed to have an interest in riding with the boys. None of the boys could figure out why they wanted to hang around them. The gang would sometimes go out of their way to get away from the girls. It was a good thing the boys could ride faster and were allowed to ride in the street. When the boys would ride down the block and the girls would see them, they would quickly catch up with them and follow them to wherever they were going. If the boys were going to the ball fields, the girls would show up and hang out there too. They would sit on the bleachers, chewing gum and braiding each other's hair and never taking their eyes off the boys, giggling the whole time. If the boys were going to the store for penny candy, the girls would go there too. If the boys were going to the playground, the girls would go there too. If the boys would go to the pool, the girls seemed to want to go swimming too. It almost seemed like the boys couldn't get away from them.

Then Hank had a great idea. When the girls would start following them, the boys would split up and go in three different directions. The girls didn't know what to think of this and would stop following along. Then the girls figured out that the boys would eventually meet back up somewhere and go to where they originally planned on going. This confounded the boys like you couldn't imagine.

So after a few times of being figured out, the boys came up with a new plan. If the girls would follow one of the split-off pairs, the pair that was being followed would just keep riding around until the girls got tired of following. This plan seemed to work better than any of the others, so that became the best play for the boys—at least for the most part it did. The plan became unraveled when a few of the boys began to take a liking to a few of the girls.

A few of the girls lived down our block and across one of the side streets, and a few more lived on the block the boys would use during the race. They must have seen the boys racing and figured out where the boys lived. They would also realize they all went to the same school in the fall, and some even went to the same church on Sunday.

The boys really had no interest whatsoever in getting to know these girls. These girls didn't like baseball, they didn't like football, they didn't like bugs or fishing, and they didn't race their bikes around the block. What in the world would they have to talk about? It didn't help the boys that a few of their sisters knew some of these girls. This gave the girls a little insight into who these boys were, and that seemed a little bit unfair. Not one of the girls had brothers the same age as the boys.

Soon the girls began to single the boys out—like a pride of lionesses on the hunt. One at a time, methodically, systematically, almost scientifically, they were able to pick a boy they liked. They would find out about the things the boy liked and then begin to do those same things he liked. It was genius. Through the boys' sisters, the girls would find out important facts that ten- and eleven- and then twelve-year-old boys at least thought were important. They found out facts like how Matthew's favorite color was green. Jimmy's favorite candy was fireballs. Bobby's favorite superhero was Batman. Hank's favorite fruit was grapes. Nate's favorite animals were whales, but his favorite was the blue whale.

The girls would use all of the facts to get to know the boys better. The boys never saw what was coming their way. It would change them a little for a few years and then change them a lot as they grew closer to being men.

ELEVEN

Meet the Girls

THE GIRLS WERE ALL IN the same grade as my Matthew. All of the girls were very nice. But sometimes they seemed very silly, and at other times, they seemed very serious. It was quite confusing to every one of the boys.

The girl who was the first one to say anything to the boys was the one who'd said, "Hi, Matthew," to my boy when they were riding by. This was Maryann, and she lived eight or nine houses right down our block on the opposite side of the street. She was tall for a girl her age. She was almost the same height as Matthew but just a little shorter. She had long dishwater-blonde hair that reached the middle of her back. Her eyes were the bluest of blue in most light but then sometimes looked like a blue gray. She had a really big attractive smile and could run faster than most boys. They would find that out later when they would play tag on the playground during recess

at school. She could run down most of the boys, as her speed was unusual for her age.

Her bike was an older secondhand bike, which seemed to break down often and had a basket on the front. One time, it would be the chain popping off, next a flat tire, and then loose handlebars or a loose kickstand. In the months and years to come, Matthew would sometimes spend more time tending to her bike than he did tending to me.

Maryann was very smart too. She would often help a lot of the kids on the block with their homework and would help them study too. She was extremely polite and charmed all of the boys' parents with her proper manners, spirit of generosity, and correct posture.

Her best friend was Elizabeth, also known as Betsy. Betsy liked to chew bubblegum and could really blow big bubbles. Her and Jimmy immediately hit it off just because of that. She had long straight hair that was as black as coal, and it reached down to the small of her back. Of all of the girls, she was the funniest of all. She didn't take things too seriously like most of her friends. She came from a big family and was the youngest of all of her sisters, and her nickname at home was "the Baby." All of her sisters were much older than her too.

Betsy also had a hand-me-down bike. It was yellow with a white basket in the front with flowers on the basket. It was much older than most bikes but not as old as Bobby's bike. Mostly everyone believed that, at one time, it was most likely her mother's.

Then there was Cathy. Cathy was the one girl who had a lot to say about everyone and about everything. She had an opinion about everything too. She thought she was smart, but not everyone shared that thought. She had short blonde hair and blue eyes. Her eyes matched her bike, the boys would say. Hank liked that but would insist that her eyes matched his bike perfectly. Her bike, like Hank's, had hand brakes but wasn't a three-speed. Hank had the only three-speed bike in the neighborhood. She had a light on her fender too, but not like Hank's. Her bike was older as well, so it must have been a secondhand bike, too, like Maryann and Betsy's.

Finally there were the twins who lived all the way at the bottom of the street. The strange thing about them was that the boys didn't realize they were twins for months, as the girls weren't always together. Joan and Jane were their proper names but everyone called them Joanie and Janie. Joanie and Janie were identical except for one thing. Janie had to wear glasses when she was in school. She had trouble seeing the chalkboard even if she was sitting in the first couple of rows. The rumor was that Joanie was older than Janie by seven minutes. The twins had golden blonde hair that was just over shoulder length and always pulled back with a hair band. They each had just a couple of freckles on their high cheekbones, and nobody could see a pattern to tell the girls apart. They would dress very similarly but always in different colors. The boys thought that was how they could tell them apart. Boy, were they wrong about that one—many times.

They had eyes that seemed green on one day and blue on others. So nobody really knew what the exact color of their eyes actually was.

There were other little things about the twins that really intrigued this young, preadolescent group of boys. If one was in a sour mood, it was a good bet her sister was as well. If one fell and scraped her knee, the other would claim she could feel it too. If one had an idea about one of the boys, the other shared the same idea before they spoke about it. They were interesting, unique, and cute, and the combination was appealing to the entire group of boys.

There was one thing in particular that drew every boy in the group to the twins. It wasn't their charming personalities. Nor was it their pretty eyes. It wasn't the fact they seemed to know what the other was thinking and could finish each other's sentences. It was one thing the boys had a common interest in that was not baseball. It was their bicycle of course. Yes, their *one* bike. It wasn't a bike they actually had to take turns riding either. As far as anyone knew, the twins were the only people in town who were lucky enough to own and ride a tandem-style bicycle. It was brand new and the only bike the boys knew of to have all chrome fenders. They thought it was one of the neatest things they have ever seen, and all of them secretly wanted to ride it. But being boys, they were too worried about being teased for riding a girls' designed tandem bike. What they didn't realize about it being a tandem, was that if there was a girl on it while they rode it, nobody would even notice it was a girl's bike. They didn't realize this for a couple of years.

Aside from the chrome fenders, this bike had all sorts of cool accessories mounted on it. First of all, it had a generator headlight system that included a red taillight as well. Nobody had that yet except for my boy. Most of the boys' lights were mounted onto either the bike front fender or the handlebars. The generator was small and mounted on part of the rear frame. And when a little lever was pushed, it would allow the generator's roller wheel to lean against the tire and spin when the tire was spinning, generating electricity that powered the front and rear light. Everyone thought it was really neat because it had a taillight and was imported from England just like my Matthew's.

Both sets of handlebars had a mirror. The front handlebars had the mirror on the right side, and the rear handlebars' mirror was mounted on the left side. Streamers emerged from the handgrips on both the front and the back. There was a bell mounted on the rear handlebars and a horn on the front. The tires had the whitest whitewalls anyone had ever seen. Also, this tandem did not have coaster brakes. It had a hand brake for the front wheel that the front seat rider could use and a hand brake on the back wheel that the back seat rider could use. Why no coaster brakes?

This tandem was not only set apart by all of the interesting and cool features; it was also a five-speed with a shifter near the front handlebars. Nobody understood that, but it made the bike so much more interesting. Also, the girl's father was able to mount a portable transistor radio underneath the back of the front seat. The girls had music (or a baseball game when they were around the boys, and that made the girls even more cool) playing whenever they wanted it. There were no less than ten amber, white, and red reflectors adorning the spokes, fenders, and pedals. It was painted a light blue, almost a silver blue color. Not one of the boys had ever seen this color before. It made the bike stand out, especially during bright and sunny days. Clearly, the tandem was in a class all by itself—much like Joanie and Janie being the only set of twins anyone knew.

TWELVE

The First Wreck, How Sweet It Was

O UR NEIGHBORHOOD, ACTUALLY OUR ENTIRE town, was a really nice place to ride around. The streets were wide, and the speed limit for cars was only twenty-five miles per hour nearly everywhere. It didn't take long to get almost anywhere in our little town. It was a very bike friendly town. Years later, the city even painted bike lanes on all of the main roads so it would be even safer for kids or anyone to ride through. All of the parks, libraries, stores, schools, pools, and plazas had bike racks to lock us to. I have heard that most towns in those years were not that far ahead in providing this for folks who rode bicycles around.

Every now and then Matthew's mother would ask him to make a quick trip to the grocery store. To get to the grocery store, which was in another part of town, there were two routes one could take. If we took the usual route that was all through the streets of town, it would take just less than fifteen minutes to get there, and most of it was uphill so the ride back was always faster than the ride there. The other way would shave off about six or seven minutes, but it was up a steep hill through this little narrow patch of woods that ran along a ridge that was nearly the entire length of our neighborhood.

The path went nearly straight up through the woods. It was about as wide as a sidewalk and covered with little, loose, round stones. Thus, everyone called it "Stony Path." Oh, it was lined with thorn-filled blackberry bushes too. The boys would take this path all of the time for many reasons. One of the main reasons was that it was the major shortcut to the grocery store, ball fields, the ice cream shop, and the little novelty or penny candy store where the boys would buy bubblegum, fireballs, pop, and baseball cards.

The return trip was always exciting and sometimes a little bit scary too. We would take the trip back to our street by riding down Stony Path, and it seemed like a challenge to see who could come down the fastest and, of course, skid at the bottom and watch the little round stones fly. It wasn't difficult for the boys to make it down the hill, as they were in complete control of the bikes and had both hands on the handlebars. So the more the boys would come down the hill without incident, the more confidence they would get. It was fun for us too, as that was part of why we bikes were made.

Stony Path seemed to never be the same twice. If we happened to go down it early in the morning, we would have to ride through a lot of spider webs that were strung across it during the night. My Matthew nearly crashed us on more than one occasion, as he loathed spider webs in his face. They never bothered me though. Sometimes the stones would be deep and loose, and my tires would sink into them, as Matthew would have to lean into the pedals and push down extra hard. Other times, the stones would be washed out from a downpour of rain, and ruts would make the path treacherous. In the early spring, the path could be frozen and slippery in the morning and then, in the afternoon, turn muddy and slippery in many spots. The little round stones seemed to be deeper toward the bottom of the hill than at the top of the hill.

The path was about as long as a football field. It started at the edge of a grassy field on the top and finished just before the end of a dead-end street at the bottom. It was such a great hill that kids and grown-ups alike would use it to go sledding in the winter when it had a deep cover of snow and ice on it. Nobody knew who did it, but the thorny blackberry bushes would be cut back just before winter would arrive to make the sledding path wider. In the spring, the bushes would fill in quite quickly. And by late July and August, they'd be full of thorns and plump sweet blackberries.

On this one particular day, Matthew's mother gave him some money and asked him to go to the store to buy a five-pound bag of sugar, as she was making apple pies and hadn't realized she was nearly out of sugar. It was that time of year too—late summer, when the apples were ready to be picked, and pies, strudels, and apple turnovers were to be baked. Matthew loved apple pie, and he was only too happy to help his mom out, as he knew he would get the first piece of pie even before it had cooled from the oven. I've heard that is the best kind.

It was also the time of year when blackberries were still in season, and blackberry pies were also a favorite in this household. His mom was one of the best bakers on the street. I assume this of course, as all of the boys would sit on the front porch and gorge themselves on many of the tasty treats she would bake. Besides, she loved to bake for the boys too. A complaint was never heard.

Matthew took the money his mother gave him for the sugar and shoved it into his jeans pocket, and we left the house. We began to take the street route but since it was late summer and already late in the afternoon, it looked like a rain shower could pop up at any time. That's how it is during August along Lake Erie's southern shores. Lake Erie is the bringer of many storms, summer and winter. At the last moment, Matthew made the decision to take Stony Path through the woods. He was strong enough now to make it all the way to the top without having to stop, get off, and walk me the rest of the way—unlike in the beginning of that first spring, when he would ride me with his shaky hands and wobbly legs.

We made it to the top with a little effort and went

on to the store for the sugar. While he was in the store, it began to rain. It wasn't heavy but enough to make the streets wet and the grass slick. No big deal, he thought, since we would be home in less than ten minutes, as we were taking the shortcut down Stony Path.

Now, the five-pound bag of sugar wasn't too heavy, but it was bulky and did cause the steering to be a little bit different. The weight shifted around and made the bag, hanging from the handlebars, swing as Matthew was pedaling. That made steering me a challenge. We came to the top of Stony Path and Matthew stopped and stared down the long, steep, and narrow length of the hill. He sat there for what seemed like an uneasy minute. The rain was beginning to pick up, and I could feel his hands wringing the hard green rubber handgrips. I thought I could feel some uneasiness in his hold on my handlebars. He took one pedal forward and stopped again. My front tire was nearly leaning over the edge of the top of the hill.

Once you got started down Stony Path, it was a commitment, and you had to go to the very end to stop. Matthew must have been nervous and realized the swinging five-pound bag of sugar, slung over my handlebars in a paper sack that had its own handles on it, was going to cause us to have problems on the dangerous hill. I think this was the only time I ever heard him say out loud that he wished he had the old milk crate basket mounted on the front of me like Bobby had on his bike. He decided to put the bag of sugar under his tucked-in shirt, just to make steering me a little easier. Confident that this was the safest thing to do, we edged over the top of the hill and began our decent down Stony Path.

Speed picks up quickly on the steep hill. No pedaling is required. But you have to be in control, or disaster is waiting for you. The first thirty yards were okay as there was less gravel and stones, but it was a bit slick from the rain. And that prevented Matthew from braking, as we would surely skid and slide.

At about the fifty-yard mark, or halfway down the path, our speed was really picking up. Beyond that was where the loose round stones began to get deeper and those changes that made up the path were most noticeable. This day, in particular, the changes were very noticeable.

To make it down the path, it was very important to keep the front wheel straight as you hit the deeper portion of stones. If you began to veer one way or the other, it was hard to get back into the straight line.

Unfortunately for us, Matthew began to veer to the left of the path. We were about at the seventy-five yard mark, where the stones were quite deep, and we were moving at a very frightening speed. We veered to the left. And when Matthew brought it back to the right to get back into the center of Stony Path, my front wheel caught some of the stones and kicked them up into my sprocket between the chain and sprocket.

If Matthew had not decided to pedal to regain control and just steered, we might have been okay. But this time, he decided to pedal through it. The stones that were caught up under my chain guard and into the teeth of my sprocket caused my chain to jump off the sprocket. With no chain, he had no control of the pedals. No control of pedals meant I had no brakes, and I couldn't stop when my pedal was slammed down hard in reverse. My front sprocket simply went into reverse and my coaster brake did not engage.

We were out of control and gaining speed every foot we traveled down Stony Path toward the dead end-street. It seems maybe a hand brake like on the twins' tandem would be a good idea?

The speed we were traveling at caused my front wheel to plunge hard into the deep stones as we neared the bottom of the hill. My tire began to vibrate and wobble to the left and then to the right. Matthew was trying to regain control and oversteered. My front wheel caught in the heavy stones and jerked my wheel completely to the right and wrenched Matthew's hands away from the slippery, rain-soaked hard green handgrips. I crashed heavily into the path and began to go into a complete tumble. Matthew was launched over the top of my handlebars.

I could hear him scream as he took sail and headed toward the right-hand side of the path. He landed hard and tumbled onto the stones and rolled into the thickest part of the late summer, thorny blackberry bushes. He came to rest on his back with the thorny branches embracing him.

As quickly as we lost control, there was complete stillness and silence except for the rain, which was now pelting Stony Path and pinging off my frame and fenders. I don't really recall if I was lying on my left side or upside down, but my front tire was pointing up the hill, still slowly rotating, and it was no longer touching the ground. I could hear Matthew moaning behind me and begin to sob a little. When he was able to get to his feet and free himself from the needlelike thorns of the blackberry bushes, he came over to me and picked me up. He straightened me to an upright position and realized my chain was off the sprocket. He didn't know how to fix me, as this was the first time something like this has happened.

When he tried to get back on me, he realized

something was very wrong. The handle bars were no longer aligned with my front wheel. Also, there was a white granular substance pouring onto my frame from underneath his now partially untucked shirt and becoming very sticky as it got wet from the rain. The bag of sugar had broken open and was now pouring all over the place. It poured onto my frame and seat, down Matthew's stomach and into his pants, and all the way down to his black high-top tennis shoes.

He was also in pain, as he was injured from the crash. He didn't realize it at first because it had happened so fast. The rain caused the sugar to get extremely sticky very quickly. He was unable to ride the rest of the way home, so he saved what sugar he could in the bag and pushed me the rest of the way home.

When he arrived at home, he parked me in the garage and slowly made his way to the house. I could see he didn't go into the house but sat on a chair near the back patio and called for his mother. The rain shower had stopped by then as he sat there soaked and began to moan. I thought I could hear him begin to cry a little.

His mother, a very caring soul, came through the back screen door and instantly realized her little boy was in pain and that something dreadful had happened. She knelt down onto one knee, took the sticky bag of sugar out of his hands, and placed it on the brick patio. She could have cared less now about baking apple pies or worrying about the sugar. She placed both of her hands softly under and around

Matthew's face and looked directly into his eyes and asked him where he was hurting. I was able to notice blood on his arms and face and noticed that some of it had run onto my handlebars as he'd pushed me home.

Then Matthew began to sob, and his mother leaned forward and took him in her arms and hugged him like only a mother could. She kissed his head and told him that everything was going to be all right and not to worry about anything. He was upset about ruining most of the sugar and crashing his favorite thing in the world. His injuries, as it were, turned out to be minor, as they were only a sprained wrist and some scrapes and scratches from being launched into the thorny blackberry bushes near the bottom of Stony Path.

After a few moments of a mother's tender loving care, he took off his shirt and shoes and blue jeans and headed into the house to get cleaned up and get some ice for his wrist and a few bandages. I, on the other hand, had to wait until tomorrow to get my tender loving care.

I, too, wasn't without injury or damage. When my front wheel had dug deep into the loose stones, it had jerked my wheel as far to the right as it could go and then just a little bit more. The "little bit more" caused my handlebars to get out of alignment with my forks by about two inches. It was not safe to ride me now. Also, my chain was not on my sprockets any longer. The stone that had gotten lodged between my front sprocket and chain had caused it to jump off. Luckily, the chain was still in one connected length, and the teeth on my front sprocket were not damaged.

Like Matthew, I, too, hadn't escaped being scratched during the crash. As I went hard into the path, the stones nicked my front fender and put a thin three-inch scratch along my chain guard. I was no longer perfect. Also, I was covered with a sweet and sticky sugar coating that hardened as I dried off during the night in the garage. I was going to need a good washing to get back to being shiny and clean like I was used to.

THIRTEEN

The Apology

THE DAY AFTER THE CRASH was a Saturday, and that meant the weekend. Matthew and his father came into the garage early in the morning to inspect the damage on his 1961 radiant-green bike built in Chicago. The doors on the old garage swung open with that familiar creak, and the bright morning sunlight hit me. It was nice and warm, as the thunderstorm from the day before had passed through quickly.

Matthew didn't say much, as he was worried his father was going to be angry about him crashing me and ruining most of the bag of sugar. His dad straightened me upright and looked to see what was really wrong with me, other than the scratches and hard white coating of sugar. Quickly, he noticed how my handlebars were not in line with my front wheel. Then he noticed how my chain was dragging on the floor of the garage. His sharp eye quickly caught the nicks and scratches too. He did not appear to be in a good mood and raised his eyebrows when he saw the damage on me. He was a quiet fellow usually and didn't really say too much. But when he did speak, it was worth listening to.

He then directed Matthew to bring him two adjustable wrenches from his toolbox. As soon as he had the tools in his hand, the mood lightened, and he began to tell his son about the many times he'd crashed his bikes when he was a kid. It was interesting to hear him, as he was a great person to listen to; he told fascinating stories. He even told Matthew that he was surprised I had stayed in such nice condition for this long.

He had learned to work on bikes just because of the many crashes he'd had when he was young. Matthew seemed much more relieved now and began to tell his father about the harrowing ride down Stony Path with a five-pound bag of sugar under his shirt in a raging thunderstorm. He told him about how he'd lost control when the chain flew off and how he'd landed in a thicket of thorny blackberry bushes. His father began to chuckle, and Matthew also began to laugh along with him.

He loosened the bolt on my gooseneck; put my front tire between his legs, holding the wheel with his knees; and explained to Matthew how to keep the wheel straight as he adjusted the handlebars to line up with the front wheel and retightened the bolt. Just like new, my wheel and handlebars were as straight as ever. Then, with no effort, he flipped me over onto my seat and handlebars. I was upside down now. He took my chain and placed the links back onto the teeth of the front sprocket and slowly turned my pedals. The chain followed along the sprocket, and in an instant, my chain was back where it belonged.

Then his dad noticed something disturbing. The chain was still very loose. That was when the man stopped doing everything, became very quiet, took a deep breath, and turned toward his son. He placed both of his large hands on his son's shoulders and looked him right in the eyes and paused for a moment as he gathered his thoughts.

Then, doing something both Matthew and me never expected, he began to apologize to his son. He felt it was his fault for the crash. Neither of us understood what he was talking about. He realized two things. One, Matthew had made a poor choice in going down Stony Path in the rain with a five-pound bag of sugar tucked under his shirt. Two, he had not taken the time to check out my chain, as he had known it would stretch and become loose over the summer as Matthew would ride me a lot this first season. It was a well-known fact that new bike chains stretched and loosened after they were broken in. Matthew's father knew that but had simply overlooked teaching his son some of the ins and outs of having a new bike and taking care of it. This he would not do again. He pulled his boy close to his large frame and gave him a big old bear hug and didn't let go too soon. His sorrow was truly felt by his boy, and the apology was accepted without question.

Then they got back to the business of getting me all fixed up and tightening my chain so it wouldn't fall off again. All the while, they were telling stories and laughing together. Our first wreck turned out to be one of the best things that happened to Matthew and his dad that summer. As it turned out, Matthew's mom was able to salvage enough sugar to make two pies and some turnovers. He would enjoy a piece of pie for dessert each night for the rest of the week.

FOURTEEN

The Camping Trips

EVERY SUMMER FOR AS LONG as I can recall, we would go on camping trips all across Ohio and the other parts of the country. We bikes would be tied to the back of a camper or sometimes to the top of the car. Matthew's dad didn't have a bike rack to put us on back in those early days. That came along later. And let me tell you, they are much nicer than being tied down on the top of a car as it zooms down the highway and around twisty-turny country roads.

I can remember the excitement in both Matthew and his sister, Erika. As soon as the plans were announced, he would begin to start piling up all of the supplies and camping gear next to me in the garage just so he wouldn't forget anything. Even with all of that preparation, he still always seemed to forget something. They'd bring tents, tarps, coolers, lanterns, sleeping bags, fishing poles, tackle boxes, baseball gloves, balls and bats, nets for catching bugs and frogs, flashlights, charcoal and lighter fluid, lawn chairs, a Frisbee, badminton, sidewalk chalk, binoculars, a transistor radio, a grill, a bocce set, and the list would go on and on. It was a wonder there was any room left for us bikes.

We would go to some of the nicest places in the state. One park might have a river with an amazing waterfall, while another might have a series of caves or a slow-moving river for long canoe trips for the family. Every park had miles of trails for either hiking or biking. Some parks might be near an amusement park or by a big lake with a long, sandy beach.

I remember the first time I was taken for a ride down a long, sandy beach on Lake Erie. My tires sank deep into the soft, wet sand, and occasionally we would venture into the waves and be swamped by water washing clear over my seat. I was always pulled out and never really in any danger of being left in the great lake. It was such an interesting experience to be somewhere so different than our own familiar little town.

Everywhere we went had a new discovery just waiting to happen. I remember when I was ridden through a stream for the first time on a camping trip. We would be left outside without a padlock, even in the rain. All of the normal rules were thrown out when we went on these amazing journeys. My boy would ride me at breakneck speed down trails and narrow paths with steep drop-offs, through creeks and other small streams, across open, grassy fields to playgrounds and swimming pools. He was allowed to ride me in complete downpours. I would be dirty for days, and the mud would stick to the treads of my whitewall tires. I didn't mind one bit being dirty. I knew my boy would give me a good wash and wax as soon as we got back home.

He would meet new friends and race all over the parks. We were allowed on all of the roads, and it was safe, as we bikes were going faster than the cars. The camping parks were huge areas with no stoplights, heavy traffic, or cars honking their horns at you to get out of the way. It was as if the roads were made just for children and their bikes.

I was parked, for the first time, in a bike rack at a state park. It was very cool—just like the ones in our town. Just my front wheel was placed between two upright bars, and it balanced me perfectly without a chance of falling over. My kickstand didn't even do that! I had fallen over many times while my kickstand was down, but not in these amazing racks at the park.

At night, the roaring campfire would reflect off of our dew-dampened fenders and chrome rims. The smoke would circle high into the trees and give the entire campground that familiar, comfortable smell of relaxation and contentment that only a campfire can. The family would sit around the fire for hours to talk, laugh, play games, and eat s'mores while his dad would pile more logs on the fire. I wondered why they didn't do that at home.

The grown-ups would sometimes tell a scary story that nearly always involved a big hairy creature from the forest, a rabid vampire bat, or a deranged and mutated human being that liked to terrorize campers. Matthew would get so scared that he would ask Erika to sit closer to him under the same blanket. Erika always tried to act like she wasn't scared by the stories, but her parents knew differently, as she would always wake one of them up in the middle of the night to walk to the restroom with her.

We would go on these amazing camping trips at different times of the summer season as well. In the early part of the summer, the sun would stay up until nearly ten o'clock and rise again before six. Those days were the best. I would be in action from just after breakfast until a thousand fireflies came out and lit up the meadows and open, grassy fields. The kids would run around with their nets and capture as many as they could and then let them go in the morning after storing them in a jar all night in the tent. I would learn this makes for a great night-light.

In the morning the songbirds would start well before the sun came up. Many times, before breakfast, we would head out very early, and the kids would take a bird book and binoculars just to see what kind of birds they could identify. We would return, and breakfast would be waiting for the group of explorers and bird-watchers. This only lasted for the early part of the summer but I'm sure would become a lifelong hobby for both Erika and Matthew.

Later in the summer, the birds wouldn't be so noticeable and would be replaced by the gentle repeating chirp of crickets. The hotter the days and nights were, the faster they would chirp. At night, the soothing sounds of a hoot owl from across the valley would make it all the way to our campsite. Occasionally one could hear the return call of another hoot owl. The brook out behind the tent would lull everyone to sleep as it bubbled and babbled and tumbled its way down to the lake and echoed the sound of bullfrogs and tree frogs.

After everyone was finally asleep, raccoons would visit our campsite and try to get into the coolers that were placed under the picnic table benches. One time, somebody forgot to properly store the coolers, and the raccoons had a feast. Buns, hot dogs, potato salad, pretzels, and eggshells were scattered all over the place. That was the only time that ever happened.

Other times, they would leave snacks out for the raccoons just to see them up close from the shelter of the tent. Another time, a raccoon who found an egg became tangled underneath me somehow and toppled me over. Oh, did it snarl and claw wildly just to free itself from underneath my back wheel. Who knew that raw eggs were the favorite snack of a wild raccoon?

I remember once, we were coming back from a fishing trip to the lake near one of the campgrounds. Matthew and his dad had caught a lot of fish, and I can still feel the cold, wet, slippery fish slapping against my frame as they hung from the stringer that was connected to my handlebars. Matthew was so excited and proud and wanted to get back quickly to show his mom. Matthew didn't seem to mind that the slimy fish was getting all over my radiant-green frame, and a few times, a few nearly got caught in my spokes as he swayed back and forth, pedaling hard to get back to his mother.

Though she was very proud of her boy, the fisherman, she despised cleaning fish. I can still hear his dad saying, "There's nothing like the smell of fresh fish frying over an open fire." Nobody was sure if his mother ever shared that same sentiment.

One thing was for sure, though. The raccoons loved the parts of the fish that weren't cooked. They would take the fish heads down to the creek and "wash" them before snacking in the evening. Their front paws looked like little hands as they cleaned the fish heads and then feasted.

Those trips were the absolute best time the family ever had during the summer. The family bonded and became closer, like families that spend a lot of time together do. The kids would become pen pals with some of the friends they would make on the longer trips, and the grown-ups would make some friendships that would last for decades. It seemed like campers were always some of the nicest people.

For me, it was a chance to help my boy experience things he would remember for a lifetime and help him become the person he grew up to be. My wheels got to travel in places many bikes never get to travel. I rode down winding mountain trails and along crystal-clear streams, across some of the most beautiful meadows and along beaches barely touched by human feet. We were taken to the places the masses didn't like to travel to. We were out in nature and among the wildlife that didn't have a problem sharing their beautiful woodland home and territory.

My family were not the kind of people who left a footprint for others to follow. When we left a place, it was cleaner than when we got there. That was one of the most endearing things about my family and my boy. They appreciated the rawness of nature and the beauty of nature left undisturbed by humankind. If they moved a twig or a rock, they replaced it, and it was not noticeable to anyone that they had gone down that path or trail.

They knew they were in Mother Nature's domain and showed her great respect and restrained from taking souvenirs and keepsakes from their trips there. Photos and memories were the only things they ever really removed from those places, besides a few fish from the streams or lakes or a seashell or two from the beaches. A few times my boy and his father would take sticks that had already fallen from trees and fashion hiking sticks for themselves. They would spend hours using a pocketknife to carve figures of animals and animal tracks into the wood. They took only things that nature had discarded and wouldn't grow back. These memories I will have for all of my existence.

FIFTEEN

The County Fair

S UMMER WAS WINDING DOWN AND the fall season was nearly upon us. The days were getting a little bit shorter and the nights just a little bit cooler. That also meant that school was about to begin again. But first, it was the Labor Day holiday weekend, and the annual county fair was in full swing. That's how one could be sure the end of summer was near. It was the last big summer event in our town that everyone seemed to go to. The entire gang went almost every day as a group until the parents wanted to go as a family, but that was usually not until Sunday. All of the boys met at one of their homes and rode out to the fairgrounds, as it was about three miles out of town.

Admission was free for all children under thirteen on the first day of the fair. The first day was always on a Wednesday, and it ran all the way until the following Labor Day Monday.

The boys had saved a lot of their allowance and chores money all summer long just to be able to have a great time at the fair. Some of the boys lived in homes where their parents couldn't always afford to give them an allowance, so other parents would create jobs to be done around their homes just so those boys could earn a little money to enjoy the fair each year. My boy's father did that for a few of his friends, like Nate, so he would be able to go with his friends. Nate's family wasn't poor, but they had to be wise with the way they spent money. So his parents struggled to afford to give Nate any extra money. We would only see them at the fair as a family, and they would still have a great time.

The boys would buy food, play carnival games, purchase ride tickets, and take rides on animals like horses, ponies, and camels. If there was any money left, they'd pick up a couple of souvenirs. Sometimes they'd go to the demolition derby, which was always held on Friday nights.

A demolition derby was when a lot of these old junky cars lined up and crashed into each other until there was only one left running. It was a spectacle for sure. We bikes would be chained to the fence right next to the track and could see the entire demolition derby. It was quite an event and the grandstands were always packed for it.

The county fair was a very special place. There were lights, sounds, and smells I had never seen, heard, or smelled before and could only experience during this time of the year. We bikes couldn't go into the fair, but the bike racks were just on the other side of the fence. And for a big part of it, we could see what went on in there. Sometimes we were locked on the racks, or sometimes we were leaning and locked to the fence. I preferred the fence, as I could see a lot more from there.

Eating food was a never-ending event when the boys went to the fair. The smells that came from the fair were absolutely amazing. Most were good; some were not. The good ones always seemed to include food. The bad ones always included animals, machines, or food that wasn't in the boys' stomachs anymore! There were barbeque pits that grilled chicken, pork ribs, sides of beef, hamburgers, hot dogs, buffalo burgers, ostrich, turkey legs, and more. My boy's favorite was the buffalo burger. He had to have one every year. Aside from the grilling pits, there were hot dog and hamburger stands everywhere. Every kind of meat was being grilled over open fires or charcoal pits. It smelled amazing!

There were French fries, cotton candy, saltwater taffy, candied apples, elephant ears, fried dough, and donuts. There were frozen bananas on a stick that were dipped in chocolate. There were Chinese food stands; Italian food stands; fried cheese stands; hot buttered corn on the cob on a stick and corn dogs on a stick; regular popcorn, cheese corn, caramel corn, and peanut carts; sausage, onion, and pepper sandwich stands and steak sandwiches stands; lemon shakes and ice cream stands; homemade fudge and soda fountains; and more! It was no wonder some kids got upset stomachs when they got off of the rides.

The rides were something special too. All had amazing lights and music coming off of them. The roar of the rides whirling around and going up and down was sometimes deafening, and that didn't include the music that went along with everything else. There were Ferris wheels, double Ferris wheels, bumper cars, a small choo-choo train that circled the entire fairgrounds, flying swings, flying umbrellas with seats, cages that took people and rotated them upside down and around, long sliding boards where the kids had to sit on burlap sacks, the scrambler, old-fashion cars on a track, crack the whip, the turtle, the centipede, the roundup (a ride that makes you stick to the wall as it spins around and then the floor drops out) tethered hot air balloon rides, and more. There were fun houses that had moving floors, moving stairs, a rotating barrel to walk through, and mirrors that could make you look large or skinny and short and tall and distorted. There were rooms with lights that made the boys' clothes glow different colors. Some of the fun houses were scary and had creepy characters inside meant to scare people. My Matthew began to go through those later on when he was a little older.

One of my boy's favorite rides was right near the fence by gate 5 (there were many gates), and I could see it perfectly. It was the double Ferris wheel. It was amazing to see when both wheels began to spin and then rotate over the top of each other. My boy's mother would never get on it, even when she was coaxed by his father. She said it just looked too dangerous. At night it was even more amazing, as there were different colored lights all around it and on each of the spokes.

Then he would ride the swings, which were attached to a tall, flat spinning wheel, and he would fly very fast, around in circles high above the ground attached only by some thin chains that seemed to be stretched outward. Only a little metal bar held him in the seat.

There are rides for people to go on that sometimes can actually make people queasy and have upset stomachs. I don't understand why they would like to do that. One year, after eating a few helpings of baked beans, Matthew went on a spinning ride that was also tilted and went up and down. All I will say is that he didn't ride it anymore after that, as he hurled those half-digested baked beans all over the place at the fair and had to stop riding me once on the way home to finish emptying his stomach. I am so glad he didn't get any on me. I have had a lot of things on me, but that would have been the worst. Personally, I think that ride gets a kick out of making people sick. Years later when telling that story to friends, he called it the "tilt-a-hurl." I totally get it.

There were some special tents that, in those times, were once called "the bizarre and unexplainable" tents. It cost extra just to go inside. There was the strongest man in the world, the strongest woman in the world, the tallest man, the shortest woman, a woman with a beard like a man, conjoined twins, sword swallowers, the world's largest horse, mutated animals, and more! There were magic shows, concerts, talent shows, art exhibits, farming equipment demonstrations, horseback riding, and trick-riding shows. There were pioneer villages with blacksmiths and musket-firing demonstrations. There were lumberjack competitions where men chopped logs with an ax as fast as they could. The lumberjacks climbed long wooden poles in a race and even did log rolling in a pool filled with water. I don't know how they did that without falling in.

Everything you can imagine happened at the county fair for one week at the end of every summer.

At night, the county fair really took on a whole new atmosphere and appearance. The late summer air was a bit cooler, and nightfall was somewhat earlier now, as autumn was truly only a few more days down the calendar. A light dew would sometimes form on my seat and fenders. In the large grass parking lot fields, some low fog would gather when the air gets cool. The clear skies caused the cooler air to condensate on the grass and other surfaces. Smoke from the barbeque pits slowly rose over the midway, rides, and animal barns and wafted its way around the grounds. I could hear the games being played and bells being rung as the winners walked away with big stuffed animals and an assortment of other prizes. Often, because some youngsters must have let them go by accident, I could see helium balloons illuminated by the lights as they floated away, only to disappear higher in the atmosphere where the darkness of the night sky overpowered the fair lights.

Crickets were making their soothing chirps again as only they can do in late summer along Lake Erie. The leaves on the trees had not turned to red, orange, and gold yet, but they seemed to look tired and ready for autumn's shorter days and cooler nights. Some of the leaves had already begun to fall.

The farmers had harvested nearly all of their fields, and the farming displays there were the jewels of the county fair. There were gourds of all shapes, colors, and sizes at the squash display. Some of the gourds and zucchinis on display were as long as or longer than the length of my frame. The big daddy and favorite of them all was the pumpkin display and competition. Some of the pumpkins were hundreds of pounds in size, and the coveted blue ribbon went to the largest and heaviest at the fair. There were orange pumpkins, white pumpkins, and green pumpkins. There were different displays of all brands of feed corn and Indian corn, squash, apples, green beans, tomatoes, potatoes, cucumbers, wheat, oats, alfalfa, and other sorts of grains. There were honey beehive displays with glass covers so people could watch the bees working.

There was animal judging, animal and tractor auctions, sheep-shearing demonstrations, cow milking twice daily, cheese judging, pie-baking competitions, food-canning competitions, local art displays, short plays, dance troupes, and musical bands playing on small stages near the junior animal barns. There were horseback-riding competitions and horse-drawn wagon judging. There was even an old tractor display, with ancient working steam engines! For no particular reason, my boy's mother just loved old red farm tractors. There were fire trucks, military equipment, civil war displays, and even a colonial village. One year, there was an antique bicycle display that every boy and his father went to, and the boys wouldn't stop talking about it for weeks. The irony now is that I feel like one of those old antique bikes.

The annual county fair wasn't only for the sights, sounds, smells, and exhibits. It's where friends would meet and enjoy being together. It's where families came together and slowed down life's hectic pace for a few days and became closer to each other. I have never heard a story told about the fair where everyone wasn't laughing about something. Those good memories sustain friendships and family ties. It's amazing how something that only comes around for a short week, once a year, has that kind of positive impact on people.

The last day of the fair arrived too soon. At the end of this night, as the boys and girls walked to their bikes or to the cars with their parents, carrying that last bag of blue-and-pink cotton candy, one more red candied or caramel-covered apple, or one more bag of popped corn, you could see them look back at the fairgrounds. They looked so they could seal in one last memory, one last vision, one last visual souvenir of lights and smoke from the open barbeque pits and French fry stands. They would take with them this visual treat until the end of next summer when the fair returned anew.

Summer was over. School would begin tomorrow.

SIXTEEN

Middle School and the Awkward Years

IT WAS MIDDLE SCHOOL NOW—THE part of the kindergarten through twelfth grade school career no child enjoys. These are the awkward years of growing and outgrowing clothing; acne and voice changes; braces; and, yes, the "P" word—puberty! School classes become more difficult too. My boy was just getting used to being one of the bigger kids in school, and now he had to be one of the younger boys again.

The school was a lot bigger too. More kids from different neighborhoods—neighborhoods that I had rarely, if ever, been to. In a smaller town like ours, you might know where everything is in town but maybe not know everybody really well. My boy Matthew was very popular but still wasn't the most well-known boy in town. There were different kids to meet and different places to see, and the school was a little bit farther away from our street too.

I remember the first time we had to go to the new middle school. James Garfield Middle School was a big school. Maybe five hundred or more children went there. It wasn't the only middle school in town, but it was the biggest. The racks for the bikes were four rows deep and the length of the entire sidewalk in front of the school.

The grades were fifth through eighth. The eighth-grade boys and girls were the big kids at school. They were one year from high school and looked and sounded much older than the kids from the younger grades. The boys looked and acted so much older that I couldn't imagine my boy ever being so big, with such a deeper voice, and maybe having some extra hair on his face. I suppose it happens, as his father had more hair on his face, chest, and back than anyone I had ever seen before—ew!

Middle school was very different. It seemed the kids were less interested in doing the fun things like marbles, red rover, tag, and hide-and-go-seek. They seemed so serious all of the time and oddly frustrated. I noticed too that they didn't seem to laugh as much. I could not understand this change I saw in all of the boys. Another thing was this— they didn't ride us bikes just to ride anymore. Not as much anyway. It's like we were used just to get from here to there or to run errands—just a mode of transportation. It was a very awkward situation, and maybe that's why these were called the awkward years, as it was awkward for everybody.

Then there were pimples, acne, or what the boys called them—zits. It was something almost every young boy and girl went through and usually started while in middle school but usually not until seventh or eighth grade—another reason to dislike those years. A few of the boys had it worse than others.

Rumors guess at what caused them—too much chocolate, not washing enough with soap, too much soda pop, too much greasy food, and so on. Nobody really knew what caused them, but all of the boys complained at one point or another that a zit showed up at the worst possible time. I couldn't help but wonder if there was ever a good time for it.

I've heard the stories. Some boys were just gross and would wait until the zit was really big, white, red, and angry-looking and then pop it on a mirror in the boys' restroom! Johnny was one for doing that all the time. That's just nasty if you ask me.

Organized socials began in middle school too. Socials were a way for the boys and girls to meet somewhere with adult supervision and learn how to socialize together. I heard, too, it was to entice the rest of the boys to get up and dance with the girls. Most of the boys hated the thought of having to go to the school gym for an organized dance—except for Hank.

Like his bike, Hank was just as flashy on the dance floor. His aunt used to be a professional dancer, and she taught him all of the dances. He was smooth too. All the girls wanted to dance with Hank. In fact, at one of the dances, a few of the teachers danced with him too! In middle school, a boy or a girl didn't have to ask anyone to go. Therefore, there was no chance of being turned down by someone you may like. Everyone could go, as the event was a sponsored by the school and chaperoned by teachers and a few parents.

One of these "social mixers" (that fifth graders were allowed to attend) was an organized square dance. Square dances were always held in the fall about a month after school began again. Square dancing was a popular thing in our town back then, and this was a good way to see what kind of social skills a young boy and young girl would have. It was even taught in gym class for a week or two. I remember the boys complaining that they couldn't play a sport and had to learn to dance. It was awkward for the kids and especially the new fifth graders. Some of the kids would be quite nervous about going, and some would be extremely excited about going. My boy was somewhere in the middle. His buddy Jimmy was always one to be ready for these socials.

Still, these socials were stressful for the kids, and that's when the zit would pop out and risk ruining a young person's self-confidence—just by residing on his or her chin, cheek, nose, or forehead where everyone could see it, like a strobe light.

SEVENTEEN

Some Major Awkward Moments

THERE ARE ALWAYS THOSE MOMENTS or little events that seem to be the things that will follow you around for life. Here are a few of the notable things that should not go unsaid in this story.

Tonsillectomy

In sixth grade, Matthew had to have his tonsils out. It could not wait until summer like it was originally planned, so it was done in the springtime. Springtime was baseball season for the middle schools and high schools. My boy was a great ball player, and when his parents and doctor decided it was time for his tonsils to come out, he was devastated. He argued and argued that it would ruin him in baseball and he'd never get a chance again to play that year.

This was when I discovered that, at this age, every dilemma or event was so much larger than life and very dramatic. He was angry, frustrated, sad, upset, and devastated. And mostly, he was not happy that his parents didn't seem to understand how he felt. There was no way for them to explain it to him so he could understand their true concerns. *Grown-ups just don't seem to care,* is what he thought. Then one day at school during gym class, his teacher (who was also the baseball head coach) heard him complaining to his friends about his parents and all of the other woes that went along with his tonsil dilemma.

The coach knew Matthew from all the way back to Little League baseball. A father himself, he let Matthew rant to his friends and then, after class was over, called him into the locker room's coach's office. He sat him down and explained how he'd overheard his concerns and complaints. Then he began to tell him a story of his own childhood. He told him about how he hadn't had parents like Matthew did and how he only had a mother, and they'd had very little in the way of money or ways to get good medical treatment when he needed it. When he'd became sick with tonsillitis, he'd almost died because he couldn't breathe due to a closed airway. He explained that my boy's parents didn't want this happening to him and only wanted the best for him so he could be the best at everything he ever tried or wanted to do.

After a while, my boy began to understand. It seemed as if he had to hear it from somebody other than his parents for the point to get across and for him to understand the love and caring his parents had for him—had always had for him.

His coach told him that, in less than two weeks after surgery, he would be back on the ball field, and his position that he played and earned would still be his. That made my boy smile, and suddenly the drama of surgery was gone.

Like the gentleman he was becoming and had always been, Matthew shook the coach's hand and thanked him. When he got home, he didn't tell anyone about his conversation with Coach Thompson but went directly in the house and hugged his mother— something middle school boys rarely did. His mother didn't ask him a thing about it but only hugged him back like only mothers can do.

And about his tonsil surgery. All went well, and he was back on the field in one week—not two.

The Corduroy Pants Incident

In the seventh grade, my boy was wearing a new pair of navy-blue corduroy pants to school. While at recess during lunch, he and some of his buddies were playing two-hand tag football. The grass was wet, but it wasn't muddy. While he was running after one of his friends, he slipped. His left leg went one way, and his right leg went the other. The events of this story have been told and retold over the years, but one thing about the story that remains unchanged is how loud the *riiiipppp* was when his navy-blue corduroy pants split from the back of his belt to just where the zipper ends in the front of his pants.

Yes, his tidy-whiteys were visible for everyone to see. His friends laughed loudly, and the entire group of kids at recess knew immediately what had happened. In twenty minutes, the entire school, as big as it was, knew about it. It was the most embarrassing moment Matthew had experienced at the middle school—so far.

He went to the office to call his mother and to see if she could bring him a new pair of pants. The phone rang and rang and rang, and nobody picked it up. The reason no one answered is still under speculation.

After Matthew had sat in the office for another fifteen minutes, terrified to walk down the hall and be laughed at by all, the office secretary had an idea. She left for a few minutes, and when she came back, she escorted him to the gym and had him change into his gym shorts. The halls were now empty, as classes had resumed.

Remember, the split was the most embarrassing thing so far. After he changed into his shorts, she escorted him all the way to the other side of the school, where the home economics classes are held. He had never been at this part of the school before this day. His eyes got bigger and bigger as he realized what was going to happen next.

The secretary brought him into the class, where no less than twenty-three seventh and eighth grade girls were staring and giggling at the sight of him in his shorts holding his trousers with the gigantic tear. It just so happened that sewing class had just begun that day. As he stood there holding his trousers, his palms began to sweat.

He had to explain to the teacher what had happened and why he couldn't contact his mother and ask if it were possible for her to mend them for him. She told him this wasn't the first time she would be asked to mend a tear, but it was a first time she would be mending such destruction of the crotch area of a pair of corduroys—all the while looking through the hole at the class as she held them up for the entire class to see the magnitude of the damage. The giggling became a low roar of laughter. Matthew's face reddened with embarrassment, and the zits that showed up a few days later were proof of it.

With this dark cloud of embarrassment and the fact he would never be able to be live it down the rest of his life, there was, as they say, a silver lining around every cloud. The home economics teacher, Ms. Stratler, did agree to have his pants mended. But she made it an extra credit project for the first volunteer of her class. Quickly in the back of the class, a hand shot up, even before her offer was completely out of her mouth.

Matthew looked to the back of the class, ever more nervous of who this young lady might be. Then suddenly, he was calm. The sweat felt cool now, and a slight smile, ever so slight, began to grow on his face.

Ms. Stratler told him to take his trousers to the young lady. He slowly walked what seemed like a mile between the rows of desks and girls looking at him, but he didn't see or feel any of the gawking stares. When he got to the last row and the desk of the volunteer who'd quickly shot up her hand, the growing smile overtook his face.

As he handed his trousers over, he gently said, "Hi, Maryann."

She smiled back and said, "Hi, Matthew."

He sat quietly and looked at nobody else as he

watched her skillfully mend his new blue corduroy trousers. In twenty minutes or so, he had a once again functional pair of navy-blue corduroy trousers. They weren't like new, but they fit just fine.

Middle school itself, aside from the awkward social and physical growing pains that kids went through, was becoming more challenging and difficult. The boys and girls had to become more independent with their schoolwork and homework. They had to strive to get good grades. They had to learn to balance time better and to organize and be punctual with assignments and projects—all of this while trying to continue being a kid, a boy, and having fun with friends and sports. And yes, at times, they would take time to ride us bikes around.

I remember Matthew and Jimmy riding around— just the two of them. I recall hearing them say that, when they are out on their two-wheeled steeds, all of the things that bother them, like school or homework or chores, just seem to melt away, and they can feel like ten-year-olds again. They had no worries or problems when they were on us, with the wind whistling through our spokes, their hair blowing in the wind—that distinct sound of winter's road gravel grinding under our tires. It was their freedom, freedom they always had when they were young and had little care in the world except for collecting baseball cards and playing at the ball field, racing bikes, and going camping. And to think that it was only a mere three years ago. How things changed so quickly when you were young.

When out on these rides, the boys would occasionally make a quick sprint and race to the next corner or to the park just to remind them of the great races and thrill of winning. It was a good time for them—these getaway rides, going nowhere but going everywhere at the same time, enjoying the quality time of life. It was something that, over the coming years, would become more difficult to find, more difficult to create, and more difficult to do.

EIGHTEEN

High School

The First Real Girlfriend

MY MATTHEW MADE IT THROUGH the awkward years of middle school just fine. Nothing that happened in middle school scarred him for life. In high school, my boy was very popular. It was said he could get along with just about anybody and had friends from many diverse backgrounds that proved this exact point. In his senior yearbook he was voted "easiest to talk to" and "easiest to get along with."

Matthew was popular with the girls too, but he really was very particular and more timid about talking to girls than anyone ever knew. Then one day during his sophomore year, a very nice girl he had been talking to for most of the year asked him to a dance! What was this madness? A girl asked a boy to a dance? In those days, it was very uncommon for a girl to ask a boy to a dance. As it were, however, there are some dances where, indeed, the girls ask the boys to a dance.

My boy was flabbergasted and, without hesitation, answered with a loud, "Yes, I would love to go!"

As I said, this girl was not a perfect stranger either, and she and Matthew had a history of sorts. She had lived in the neighborhood when they were both young and in grade school but moved away just after seventh grade when her father's work transferred him to a new town.

Now she was back and she and Matthew picked right up with each other. They would sit on the front porch steps of his house and talk for hours about anything and everything. Nothing seemed to be off limits with these two, and they even discussed some of the more embarrassing personal stuff that teenagers go through.

She was the girl who had first said hello to him when the girls would ride bikes past the boys. Yes, this was Maryann, with the long hair down to the middle of her back and the seamstress who had repaired his dark-blue corduroy pants in seventh grade. Perhaps the familiarity was what made it so easy for Matthew to talk to her—or maybe it was something else. They sure seemed to hit it off right away, as they would walk to school quite often when it was too cold out to ride their bikes. They would talk all of the way there or until they saw their other friends.

Remember Maryann's old second-hand bike that used to break down all of the time? Well, she didn't have that anymore. She had a brand-new women's automatic three-speed. It was as beautiful a bike as she was a nice young lady. It was made in England and seemed to have a bit of class to it. It was black with white pin stripes and a white tipped-back fender that had a nice round reflector attached to it. The frame had raised engravings and designs. The seat was all leather with springs for support, and it even had a long aluminum air pump attached right on the long part of the frame. (I guess her parents remembered the old bike breaking down a lot.) On the handlebars was a bell just like mine and an electric horn. The horn was awesome too. It was in a shiny chrome case that held one big battery and was honked by pressing a tiny black button near the left handgrip. She had not only a headlight but also a taillight that was powered by a generator attached to the rear frame. The sprocket even had the silhouette of a goose as part of it. It was classy all the way around.

Maryann had grown into a striking young lady and still had the long hair down the middle of her back but now with a little curl added to it. Her brilliant blue eyes and high cheekbones made her look like a fashion magazine model. She had very nice posture and held her head high as she walked. She wore a different sweater every day in the fall with a white blouse on underneath. She liked to wear skirts, but when she would ride her bike over to our house, she would wear jeans and saddle shoes like most of the other girls wore in those days. She would put her hair in a ponytail with a rubber band that matched the color of her sweater. Matthew was very fond of those sweaters. She wore makeup, too, but not enough to cover up her natural beauty—only a little blue eye shadow and pink strawberry or cherry lip gloss. No fake eyelashes like some of the girls. Her eyes were already beautiful, and nothing could enhance them. Her fingernails were never polished with a color but with a clear polish that made them shine anyway. On one finger, she wore a blue star sapphire ring her grandmother had given her some years ago. It was set in a gold band and looked great on her hand. On the cooler fall days, when it was almost too cool to ride me, they would go for the longest walks and have great conversations.

I could hear the conversations my boy would have with his buddy Jimmy about the upcoming dance, and boy was he nervous. He really liked Maryann and didn't want to blow it. He was afraid, too, because she was such a good friend, and he didn't want to ruin that part of their relationship. He was nervous because he had to meet the parents before he was permitted to take her to the dance. He had met them long ago when he was a little boy, but now he was in high school; and his voice had changed, and he was as tall as most grown-ups.

I remember the meeting very well as he rode me to her house for the big meeting with the parents. Halloween had passed, and it was well into November, but it was an unusually warm month that year. Normally, the weather for that time of the year could be quite cold. But Lake Erie's water was still quite warm, so it kept the chill out of the air. There were years when I was already put away for the winter by then. That wasn't the case this year. It was warm and dry, and he rode me the near mile to her house. We got there quickly, as it was almost entirely downhill from our house to her house.

As I hear it told, my boy had to be there around 6:30 in the evening, just after dinner, and it was already dark outside. In the cooling night air, I was parked on the brick walk that was just in front of the flower beds. He was wearing blue jeans, a green and gray checkered flannel shirt, and black high-top basketball shoes. Those were in fashion for boys in the tenth grade back then. I could tell he was nervous because his hands were very sweaty and slipping on my green rubber handlebar grips. When he pedaled to her house, his legs didn't have his normal steady strength, and I could almost feel some hesitation with every pump of the pedal.

He walked up the five steps of the brightly lit front porch. He knocked on the door, and Maryann opened the door nearly the instant the last knock could be heard. She was smiling and quickly pulled the door closed behind her and stepped outside. She pulled him down the five steps by his untucked flannel shirt and back into the less well-lit part of the driveway. For a fleeting moment, he thought the meeting was off.

No such luck for my boy this night. Smiling from ear to ear, she told him to tuck in his shirt and take a few deep breaths and that there was absolutely nothing to worry about; this would only take a couple of minutes. Her parents simply wanted to meet him since they were going on a date.

A DATE he thought! Then quickly, he realized that was exactly what this dance was. Suddenly, he looked at Maryann a bit differently, as that's what happens when the heart gets involved. He was going on a date with one of his best friends, who just happened to be beautiful and someone he could talk to about anything. A date, and now he had to meet the parents. How would this go? He couldn't help but wonder as he was tucking in his shirt and barely hearing a word Maryann was saying.

Instead of going into the house by the front porch, Maryann led Matthew around the side of the house to the side door that entered into the kitchen. The kitchen seemed to be less formal and more comfortable for everyone. She knew this, as her parents wanted to meet in the living room. They sat down at the kitchen table, and she offered him a glass of milk and some cookies. He was still full from his own dinner and had barely digested anything yet due to his nervousness about the event. But still he accepted the milk and cookies out of politeness.

He had just bitten into the first of the homemade chocolate chip cookie when both her mother and father entered the room unannounced. With a near mouthful of moist chocolate chip cookie, he stood up, bumped the table, and nearly knocked over his glass of milk. Without thinking he quickly wiped his right hand on his jeans and swallowed the half-chewed bite of cookie. He stuck out his hand and said hello to Mr. and Mrs. Smythe. Barbara and Richard were their first names. Young people in those days were always polite and formal.

Mr. Smythe grabbed my boy's somewhat still sweaty hand and gave it a firm handshake. Mrs. Smythe commented about how long it had been since she has seen him last, as he had been just a small boy then. "My how you have grown" she said. "Richard dear, he is nearly as tall as you."

Mr. and Mrs. Smythe were very well-spoken people and spoken well of as well. They were members of the church and involved in many different community organizations. Matthew didn't know it, but his father and Mr. Smythe had been in the military together after high school and before college.

Mrs. Smythe looked at Maryann and motioned to the living room. She told Matthew to leave his milk and cookies, as this wouldn't take very long. He and Maryann joined the Smythes in the very large living room, where there was a fire blazing in the fireplace. The parents sat in identical high-backed chairs that faced the sofa where both Matthew and Maryann had sat down. Mr. Smythe excused himself for a moment to get a glass of water.

Matthew noticed that Maryann had sat down so close that their legs were actually touching each other. He felt even more uncomfortable now. His hands were folded on his lap, and he had no intention of unfolding them, worried Maryann may grab hold of the one closest to her. Not only was he wearing a flannel shirt, it was warm out, there was a fire in the fireplace, and now his leg was touching Maryann's leg; and he began to perspire on the back of his neck. This was most likely not as much due to heat but to nerves, as he had never been in a situation like this one ever before. Would there be more zits in a few days?

Mrs. Smythe's eyes never left him, and she fired the first salvo of questions that were really nothing more than icebreakers to loosen up the mood and the atmosphere. First she said that she noticed he wasn't wearing navy-blue corduroy trousers.

Maryann gave her a stern look, and before she could say anything to her mother, Mrs. Smythe asked how his family was doing and if they still lived in the house near the bottom of the hill.

Matthew knew she knew all of this already, as they belonged to the same church still. My boy answered all of the yes-or-no questions with a polite, "Yes, ma'am," or, "No, ma'am."

Then Mr. Smythe asked what kind of sports he liked and if he played any sports. Baseball was the answer, and Matthew added that he would like to run track, but the seasons conflicted and overlapped each other. It just so happened that Mr. Smythe had played minor-league ball while he was in college. He said he kept waiting and hoping for the big leagues to call him up, but it had never happened. Then when he met Mrs. Smythe, his focus had changed, and he'd gotten out of baseball. Still, it was a nice thing to have in common, Matthew thought.

The conversation went back and forth like that for about fifteen minutes until the more serious questions came up. Matthew was a little more relaxed at this point but still very warm, and he could feel the sweat finding its way down his back.

Mrs. Smythe asked the first one. "Tell me, Matthew, have you ever dated anyone before?"

Embarrassed, he told her, "No, ma'am."

And before he could breathe, she asked, "What do you think of our Maryann?"

This time he paused for a moment, as he wanted to get the answer just right. After a moment, he felt Maryann's leg gently press against his, undetectable by her parents, and he turned and looked at Maryann while answering Mrs. Smythe's question. "Mrs. Smythe, I think your daughter is great, and I can talk to her about anything."

He turned to Mrs. Smythe, looked her right in the

eye without blinking, and continued, "I don't know any other girl like her."

Mrs. Smythe straightened in her chair and began to speak but was quickly cut off by her husband as he began to get out of his chair and grabbed his wife's hand saying, "Well, I have heard all I need to hear. Son, how will you be getting to the dance? Be sure to have Maryann home by ... let's say 11:30, shall we?"

Matthew stood up directly and answered that they would be riding with Jimmy and his date, as Jimmy was eight months older and already had his license.

"That's fine with me my boy, fine with me. Now come, dear, and let's leave these two alone for now."

They shook hands, and Mr. Smythe and a rattled Mrs. Smythe left the two sweethearts alone in the warm room. They sat back down on the couch. Breathing a sigh of relief, Matthew looked at his watch. It was 7:45 p.m., and they had nearly been in there for an hour. "A few minutes you said." With a grin, he looked at Maryann. His back was now soaked with nervous perspiration which was going to make his ride home a chilly one.

Maryann looked at him with that smile and those blue eyes and said, "I'm great? You have never met anyone like me? You can talk to me about anything?"

That, I found out, was just what girls liked to hear. Before he could answer, she grabbed his hand, interlocked her fingers with his, and planted a big kiss right on his cheek and gave him a hug that seemed to last longer than most.

They sat on the couch for another hour before he had to be home, as it was a school night and he had a curfew. They forgot all about the milk and cookies. She walked him to his bike. This time, she wasn't smiling, and he wanted to know what was wrong.

She said, "Don't you know?"

In the darkness, he told her he did not. The porch light was not on now. She said she was going to miss him until tomorrow, and she grabbed his face with both of her soft hands and gave him his first proper kiss on the lips and then ran into the house. It was a perfect, not to short and not too long, sweet, warm, tender kiss on the lips. He could taste the strawberry lip gloss the whole way home, and that made the ride home a little bit warmer.

Lucky me, I heard every last word of their conversation as two of the front windows were open, since it was more like a cool summer night instead of autumn. Tonight began a great romance. And Matthew would remember the taste of her lip gloss as long I can recall.

NINETEEN

High School Ups and Downs

BEING THAT MATTHEW AND MARYANN where so young when they began dating, the relationship only lasted a year before they decided to see other people. It wasn't an ugly breakup, but still he was very devastated. He would still talk to her, but the long walks and the long conversations came to a halt near the middle of eleventh grade.

He didn't date anyone else for what seemed like a long time. All of the guys had steady girlfriends except for my boy. I mean, he had dates but none that he put the effort into like he had with Maryann. He went to dances with these other girls and would see Maryann with other dates too. He admitted to Jimmy, his closest confidant, that it really bothered him to see her with other dates. Jimmy wanted to intervene and go talk to Maryann about it but decided not to, as my boy told him to never say a word. Jimmy, a great friend, respected that. And not once did Jimmy say anything to her about how Matthew's heart still belonged to her—even if she didn't realize it. That's the way it stayed—for now.

Another thing in high school that seemed like an emotional roller coaster was all of the different teachers Matthew would have over the four years. Some were the best he ever had, and others were the worst he ever had. He would have one great teacher in one period and then a horrible teacher in the next. It's not that they were always bad at what they taught; sometimes it was that their personalities didn't seem to click with the kids in school. Some teachers didn't like athletes as students, and then others didn't seem to care for the popular kids or the really bright students. Some didn't always fancy the kids who couldn't afford stylish clothing or keep up with the latest fashions.

Some of the teachers didn't care for the kids who had to struggle to get average grades. They simply felt these kids weren't trying hard enough. In many cases, these teachers didn't know the kinds of lives a lot of these kids had at home. Some came from broken homes, where the parents were no longer together, or a parent may have passed away. Some of the kids had stepparents they didn't get along with, and that was sometimes very stressful. Some of the kids had to take the place of a parent and not only grow up themselves but also help their younger brothers and sisters through school and growing up.

Many of the teachers were near the end of their

careers, too, and just wanted to be finished with teaching all together. So they didn't put a lot of positive energy into their classes.

Then there were the teachers who thought they were the police of the school. They weren't looking for what the boys and girls were doing right. Instead, they were always looking for something they were doing wrong. Don't be tardy. Don't talk in class. Don't chew gum in school. Don't hold hands in the hallway. Don't get caught kissing in school. Don't cut across the grass with your bike. Don't cheat on quizzes or tests. And worst of all, no fighting or swearing.

If you got caught doing any of these you risked getting a detention, which meant you had to stay after the school day was over or come in one hour before school began. It was rare when a student could make it through the entire four years of high school without getting at least one detention. The detentions went on that year's record but didn't follow them after high school. Some kids spent more time in detention than in many of their classes for the semester.

Some of the boys from the group, like Johnny, seemed to like getting detentions. Nobody really knew why at the time. But by the end of high school, he came to respect the teachers and became friends with a lot of them—so much so that he decided he would like to become a teacher someday. *Nobody* but *nobody* saw that coming. It turns out that Johnny came from one of those broken homes and then had a stepdad who didn't like him at all. So, getting to school earlier or staying later was better than going home on time most days.

The whole thing about all of these different teachers was this, I guess: Teachers where people, too, just like the kids were kids. They had feelings, opinions, and sometimes good and sometimes bad attitudes. Some days were good days and some days were bad days. Everyone was different, and those differences were what made everyone learn how to get along with everyone else. It was too bad, but these lessons seemed to only be figured out or realized long after high school was finished.

TWENTY

College! Go Team!

NOT LONG AFTER MY BOY graduated high school, he was headed off to college in the middle of the state somewhere. The car was loaded with all that he could take with him, and I was put on the bike rack on the back of the car. I thought we were going on another camping trip, and I thought it was odd that I was the only bike to be going. I had no idea we were heading off on our own four-year adventure.

Matthew took me with him, as the campus was bigger than our entire town, and he would need a way to get around. He rode me everywhere that first year. The part I didn't care for at all was the fact that I had to be parked outside on a rack with a lock around me in all sorts of weather. It was terrible. I was rained on, hailed on, snowed on, and baked in the sunlight. And once, I was nearly struck by lightning! My chain rusted, and my rims began to pit with rust too.

Matthew seemed to forget about all of the importance of mechanical care his father had instilled in him when he was at home. Rarely was I washed and waxed to the high gloss I had been accustomed to my entire existence. It seemed as if Matthew just didn't think about me as much as he had before. Still, I thought he would have taken better care of me like he had all of the years we lived at home and I was able to be in the garage when the weather wasn't good enough to ride in. He didn't take the time or make any effort, and the harsh Midwest weather really took a toll on me.

I couldn't blame him though, as he always seemed to be in a big hurry and carried a lot of books with him every time we rode across the campus. The stress of college was quite clear.

We began in the fall, when the weather was still nice. College was totally awesome in the fall. I met so many other bikes from all over the country and all over the world. No cars were on the campus streets, just bikes, along with throngs of young people, walking, riding, or running to class.

For ten weeks during autumn, almost every campus had football fever, and this campus was the king of that. Thousands of students and former students and parents would swarm the parking lots and ovals on game day. The stadium was gigantic and held just over one hundred thousand screaming fans. They would have the biggest picnic you would ever see all the while, wearing the colors of the school, which were scarlet and gray. Many not so nice things were said about the other team too—especially a team from that state up north. I have no idea what that state is.

There would be bonfires, singing, grilling, and parking lot football games. It didn't matter what the weather was like on these Saturday afternoons. These fans were full of energy and spirit. I was once hit square on my front fender by an errant football throw from some girl. Matthew had to bend my fender back into shape for the ride back to his dorm at the end of the festivities. At least she didn't hit my headlight. It was such an exciting time—until the snow began to fall.

During his college years, Matthew began to write letters to Maryann, and they struck up an amazing long-distance relationship all through the United States Postal Service. They would write all the time. Once while they were home in the summer, he asked her out, and his heart finally healed. I could see it in his face and hear it his voice when he would talk about her to his still best friend Jimmy. He and Maryann even went on a few bike rides while they were home. It felt good for all of us.

He started dating Maryann again, even though she went to a different school than we did. I had missed riding with her and her bike. I hadn't seen her bike except a few times during those breaks. I thought about how I remembered her first bike being an older second-hand bike that Matthew would spend time fixing and making sure the chain would not pop off. Now, I was an older bike with more miles and dents and scratches than her three-speed automatic would ever see. Her bike was still in great shape, as it stayed home while she was away. I should have noticed, but I didn't, that my days were slowly slipping away. And I had not an inkling of what my next twenty-five or so years would bring.

TWENTY-ONE

College is Over

W E DID THIS SAME ROUTINE for nearly four years. During Matthew's last spring break, he took me home and parked me in the garage with the other bikes and garage inhabitants. It felt so good to be home again, even if I was not the same shining, radiant-green boy's two-wheeler I had been when we first went to college. I was not new any longer. I will say that, during his summers at home, he would wash me, oil my chain, and tighten all of the nuts and bolts he could. I would even get a good wax job sometimes. Still, the years were clearly beginning to show on me. The long winters along the great lake didn't treat chrome and steel very well. Being locked to a bike rack for months on end with snow, freezing rain, and every other kind of moisture there is was certainly not a fun time for a bike that was made to be ridden.

Still, I considered myself very lucky. When we

would go back to college after a long summer break, I would see some of the same bikes that hadn't moved since the previous year. Some were still locked to a rack with flat tires, broken spokes, missing wheels, and chains so rusted they would never work again. They had been abandoned forever. I, at least, was lucky to return to the comfort of our old garage and be out of the weather and brutality of a strange place, where not everyone likes or respected their childhood "freedom machines."

I had scratches and scrapes and dents. Many of the scratches were beginning to rust, and my tires were not as good as they could be, but they still held air. At least he stopped skidding as he got older. It had been a full three years since I had gotten a new pair of tires.

Matthew didn't ride me very much during his breaks from college. He was older now, and he drove the family car when his father would allow him to. Or he would catch a lift from friends.

For some reason, however, this time when spring break was over, he didn't take me back with him. I thought this was very strange.

TWENTY-TWO

My Last Ride, and I Didn't Even Know It

I HAD BEEN IN ONE OF my extended periods in the garage when, all of a sudden, the door swings open, and it's my boy, who is now a grown man for sure and a college graduate. He was finally home for good from college. For at least I thought he was anyway. His time away at school has seemed like an eternity, except for the few three and a half years I had spent there with him. Something seemed different about him this time.

He took me away from the other bikes in the garage and put my kickstand down and knelt down on one knee. He felt to see if my tires were inflated enough to go for a ride. They were, barely, as he was much bigger than the young boy who had first taken me down the block. He took a quick look at my chain to make sure it was not too loose. His memory of the

Stony Path crash never was far from his mind when he wanted to take me for a ride.

He turned me into the driveway, threw his right leg over my seat, and placed his left foot on my pedal and pushed off; and we moved down the now cracked and broken pavement of the old driveway. I creaked under his adult weight, and my tires made a strange rubbing sound on the forks and fenders. You see, it turns out they needed more air after all.

We turned left out of the driveway, just as we had when we took our first ride more than a dozen years ago. His grip was so much stronger than I remember, even when he was in high school just a few years ago. The cracks in the sidewalks were so much bigger now than they had been then. The trees, too, were much larger and cast larger shadows on all of the yards, and the tree's roots pushed the sidewalk up into uneven squares. We went past many of his friend's homes, but there was no yelling with excitement this time. His friends had all moved away after they'd graduated college. The neighborhood was not nearly as loud as it had once been. Like the kids, the neighborhood had matured and had quieted down and seemed almost too quiet and peaceful. It wasn't as alive as it had been when we were racing around the block or avoiding the girls.

That brought instant fear and an uneasy anxiousness to me. What had happened to all of my friends? Were they, too, enduring long spells in their garages and not being ridden either? Were they still there at all? There were stories of some of the boys and girls growing up and selling their bikes to other kids in different neighborhoods. That knowledge didn't fill me with good feelings.

But here I was again, whizzing down our block to a sudden stop that ended with a long skid on the sidewalk. I guess I had one more skid left in that old tire after all, and this was the perfect place for it. I missed the excitement and the thrill of exploring all of those places we would visit. I missed the races we would have around the block and the times we tried to lose the girls, who would follow us to the ball fields or the candy store. That hadn't happened for a long time now. Things were different now, and we were all alone on this ride—just my Matthew and me.

We made a turn at the end of the block and headed for the path that cut through the woods, Stony Path. It had been a long time since we had been on this path. When Matthew was in high school, he'd learned to drive a car, and he didn't need to take the shortcuts through the woods to go to the store for his mother. If he needed to run an errand, he would take the car, and our time together began to become less and less.

Now, I rarely got the chance to be ridden. My tires slowly deflated as I sat parked in the garage with all of the tools, the wheelbarrow, the mower, the snow blower, the sleds and boxes, and the other bikes that had become my "family" these past twelve or more years.

But now I was being ridden again by my boy, and I could feel his energy and the memories surging through his legs and hands as we flew down the familiar roads of our town. We were onto Stony Path now, and he rode me up it so fast this time. Never had we made it up that hill so quickly.

After we crested the top of the path, he rode me across the grassy field to the candy store. He only stopped in for a few minutes to say hello to the owner, who he'd known his entire life. I was parked outside on the parking lot that had old wads of gum flattened into the pavement. It used to get stuck to my kickstand when we would come here during the hot summers and my kickstand would sink into the gum encrusted blacktop.

When we left, we headed back across the grassy field, toward Stony Path. This time, as we approached the crest of the hill, we weren't slowing down like we always did.

We always stopped at the top to peer over the edge, pick out our route on the path, and then let gravity pull my front tire off the edge to begin what, many times, was a scary ride down the loose stony trail. This time, we hit the edge going quite fast, and he launched us over the top of the hill. For the first time in my existence, both of my tires were not touching the ground while someone was riding me. I saw the land quickly fall away as we were in midair over the path. We landed on my back wheel first. When my front wheel hit the path about thirty feet down from the takeoff at the top of the hill, he pedaled faster and faster. We descended down Stony Path at a frightening speed.

My tires coursed through the loose gravel, and I

could feel my front tire begin to dig in and thought perhaps he was losing control again like on the one fateful August afternoon many years ago.

Then suddenly, he pushed down on my pedal extra hard and pulled my handlebars up with great force. My tire was pulled free of the death stones, and he was again in complete control. The tiny stones were hitting the underside of my fenders, making that familiar metallic *tink* when they hit.

We made it to the bottom of the hill, and he slammed on the brakes and slid my rear tire out to the side, with a shower of little stones flying high into the air and landing on the pavement of the dead-end street where the path ended. My rear tire was about a foot away from the dreaded thorny blackberry bushes.

He let out a triumphant shout, "*Yeah*! I have always wanted to do that!"

I, on the other hand, had not. Yet it was another first for me and my boy. So many firsts we have had.

Finally he steered me over the curb and onto the dead-end street, and we headed for home but at a much slower pace now. He steered me back and forth across the street in lazy half-moon arcs, as there was no traffic to be seen on this late Sunday afternoon. We took sweeping, long, low turns, where more of the side of my whitewall tires was touching the road than the treads. It felt as if we were going to fall completely over on my side, but we didn't.

We made our way back to our crumbling driveway, and he parked me on the sidewalk leading up to the house. He put my kickstand down and sat on the painted green stone porch steps. He pulled me close to take a good long look at me. He ran his hands along my fenders and remark about every scratch and tiny dent he felt. Talking to himself, it was as if he was cataloging in his mind the memories we had made together.

There were so many memories. I had been with him through thirteen springs, thirteen summers, and thirteen fall seasons. I had been with him through six baseball teams, sixteen camping trips, countless races, five different girlfriends (one he dated twice and still did), thousands of trips to school, hundreds of trips to the candy store and ball fields, and too many trips to count up and down Stony Path.

We'd been through four tires on the back and two tires on the front. We'd been through two broken mirrors and one broken horn and had lost one reflector too. We'd been through fourteen crashes (wipeouts as he would call them)—two bad ones that he would remember due to the scars that are reminders on his legs.

I heard him say to me, "We've had some great times, haven't we, old-timer? You've been with me through thick and thin as I grew up. You are a great bike, the best ever."

Then he stood up, grabbed my handlebars, steered me onto the driveway, and walked me toward the garage. It seemed like a long walk back to the garage this time. He opened the door and slowly rolled me over next to the silver blue tandem his parents used to ride all the time. He put my kickstand down and gently leaned me onto it. He ran shirtsleeve across my headlight to clean off some dust and patted my seat. He turned away and said, "See you around."

As he closed the door, I heard the padlock click locked, and I rested on my kick stand. I saw the other things around me, already with a thick coat of dust and neglect. With sudden realization, I thought, *This is most likely my future.* I certainly hoped not, but I was now unsure.

I could hear his footsteps slowly fade away as he headed down the driveway toward the house. The garage became very quiet and still. How long would it be until he came back for me? How long before he would ride me once again and we'd have those same kinds of thrills we'd had this afternoon?

It was so quiet in here now—lonely too. Was this to be my last ride?

TWENTY-THREE

The Cleanup

IT WAS SUMMER AGAIN. IT was my twenty-fifth or thirtieth year—I couldn't recall—without anyone around to look at me or even think about riding me ever again. My wheels hadn't turned in ages. My tires were flat and the rubber was dry-rotted. My once-sparkling, shiny chrome rims and handlebars were now a pitted, rusting mess that no longer reflected light. The loud horn that Santa put on me that first Christmas, which made dogs bark and cats run, had long been broken and discarded. I hadn't felt the grasp on my handlebars and tennis shoes on my pedals in I couldn't recall how long. No wind had whistled through my spokes in what seemed like a lifetime now, and my light hadn't lit the way on a darkened street or alley for way over a decade. It was humid and hot in the garage. Cobwebs were everywhere, and spiders had made a maze of webs throughout my frame.

Then suddenly there was a familiar noise I hadn't heard for a very long time outside the garage. It was my owner's mother. She was talking to someone. I could hear her say that she was moving away and couldn't take anything in the garage with her. As much as she would love to take her bikes, she couldn't. Everything in the garage needed to go.

Here it comes, I thought. Finally, I was going to realize my worst fear. I felt I was heading to the curb, and this was probably the end for me and my other garage companions. We all knew it. It was only a matter of time.

The other voices I heard were those of much younger people. It was two boys in their teens. I could hear the lock being unlocked. Then the old barn-style doors of the garage swung open, and for the first time in a long time—with that old familiar squeak and creak of the hinges—there was sunlight and fresh air in the garage. It instantly made me remember what it was like when I was in here and those doors would open on a hot, sunny summer day, and my boy would sling his baseball glove over my handle bar, and we would be off to the ball field for the rest of the day. He would lean me against the backstop fence, and I would hear boys playing baseball all day. But alas, it was not then; it was now. And my fate was surely sealed for the worse.

The two young strangers entered the tightly packed garage and were amazed at the volume of things in here. They were dreading the "cleanup," as they called it. These were young boys of a different generation, a different and more modern era. And they wouldn't want anything to do with a bike as old and worn out as me. Surely they would only want something new and shiny and probably couldn't appreciate how I was made in a different time. I was low-tech by the current day's standards. Besides, they were old enough to drive cars and had no need for an old, rusty, broken-down, neglected, radiant-green boy's two-wheeler with coaster brakes.

I was not alone in this sad fate. My boy's parents became avid cyclists after Matthew and his sister moved out. They never bothered with me though. They bought new bikes of all varieties for themselves. Now, only his mother remained, and she was much older and unable to ride like she did before.

Next to me was an old silver-blue five-speed tandem. Remember Janie and Joanie's tandem?

This was it. My boy's parents bought it from them when they were finished with college. Next to her was a newer bike that could be folded in half and had smaller wheels. Along the back was a fine fellow from England, whom we called Winston. He was special. Finely tuned with ten gears, Winston was once used for racing in another era. The stories he told us were exciting. Next to Winston was another tandem that was in very bad shape—bent rims, missing rear seat, rusted chain, broken kickstand, broken light, and probably more, but I couldn't see it all from my spot in the garage.

Erika's bike had been gone for decades. She took her with her when she moved out after she was married. I wondered how she was doing these days and if she still had her old bike.

All of their stories are interesting and unique, but they were not like mine. Of all of these bikes, I was the first to come here. I knew all of the history here from the beginning. I had seen my owner and his family come and go. Now, I was afraid all of us would share the same fate. Or at least it seemed that way that day.

The two boys waded through the rest of the belongings in the garage and finally made their way to me and my companions. I was shocked to hear how the tone of their voices changed and the familiar energy they used in moving things out of the way to get to me and my friends.

"Look at all of those old bikes!"

Could it be true? I was now anxiously but very cautiously optimistic. Was it possible they could have some appreciation for the classics? The one boy with blond hair and blue eyes saw me and gently pulled me from the pile. His hands on my handlebars had that familiar feeling. My wheels were turning, and I was being steered out of the garage into the bright sunlight. With a squeak, my kickstand was put down, and I was again leaning on my own. The warm blacktop felt so good on my flat tires. He told his friend, in an excited tone, how cool this old bike looked.

Then the magic to my ears came from my owner's mother. She asked, "Do you boys like bicycles?"

They were so quick to respond. "Are you kidding? We love bicycles, and my dad would just love to see this old bike right here. He's been looking for one as long as I can remember."

Matthew's mother was elated to hear that. In a moment of near tearful passion and thoughtful generosity, she told the boys to take however many of the bikes they wanted, as long as they would go to a good home and would be used again like they had been in the past.

They were flabbergasted at the idea of being able to take as many of these old bikes as they wanted. Quickly, they were picking which of us they wanted and who was going to get which bike. As a surprise, I was to be given to the blond boy's father. The tandem that had been leaning on me for the past eight summers was going to the same place as well. Winston was going to the other boy's house, and so was a newer mountain bike. The folding bike was going to the blond-haired boy's sister, as she had a love of folding bikes. In all, seven of us were leaving this muggy, dusty, rusty, and dirty place for what we hoped was a new beginning.

Perhaps we could return somehow to those glorious days with an owner that would once again appreciate us and use us as we were intended. Perhaps we could fly down hills again, spend the day at the ball fields, go for rides in the park on the dirt trails, race around the block, spend a week camping in a national park, or make the nighttime run in record time to beat curfew after leaving a girlfriend's house.

How nice it would be to be waxed and shiny again—to have a boy shake with excitement when he took hold of my handlebars and wonder if he was big enough to ride me. How glorious it would be for even half of that to happen to us once again.

TWENTY-FOUR

Where Are We Going?

NIGHT HAD FALLEN BY THE time the boys were finally finished with the cleanup. One by one, we were rolled out of the garage and piled into the back of a truck to be taken to our new homes. Where they would be, we couldn't help but wonder. How far away were we going? And who would want to have us in the shape we were in? The breeze from riding in the back of the truck brought back distant memories of what it once was like to cruise through the streets of this town. It was a feeling that brought us back to the days of feeling needed … worthy … important. We were nervously excited. It was a much shorter trip than we thought it would be. It was only a several blocks away from our old home!

The boys were excited to tell their parents about how they fell into such good fortune. I could hear them as they brought out the father of the blond-haired boy. They'd blindfolded him, and they were telling him they had something for him that he was absolutely going to love. Oh, how I hoped so!

He stood there under the glow of a streetlight, with the blindfold over his eyes, as the boys quietly and carefully took me out of the back of the truck. My tires, completely flat from dry rot and neglect, didn't shield my rims from the rough, hard concrete sidewalk. With a loud squeak, the blond-haired boy put my kickstand down and parked me on the sidewalk. Then he told his father to take off the blindfold and open his eyes.

The man pulled the blindfold off, rubbed his eyes, and looked my way. At first, he wasn't sure what to make of this. He walked around me, looking me up and down and, with a keen eye, assessing the shape I was in.

But it was when he grabbed my handlebars that I could feel that familiar energy that once was there when a young boy first clutched those very same hard dark-green handgrips on that snowy Christmas morning. He was more than amazed. He was really excited. I could feel how thankful he was to his son and his friend.

With a childlike smile, he asked his son, "Matthew, are you sure this is for me?"

Wait, did he say Matthew? It couldn't be of course. He was too young. This boy's father was actually younger than my Matthew from yesteryear. Was this some mystical joke or some ironic coincidence? I thought maybe it was both, and I didn't care.

Matthew replied, "It's all yours, Dad. I know you have been wanting a bike like this for as long as I can remember." Matthew's dad gave his son a long hug and thanked him.

On two flat tires, I was rolled down the long driveway and into a garage that had very familiar doors. The lights were turned on, and there were newer bikes there too. I was quickly placed in the center of the garage and given a very thorough inspection. The boy's father was thinking out loud. I could hear him say, "Oh, I think you will clean up just fine," and, "I can't wait to get started on you."

Then I heard it as he tilted me away to look down at my rusting sprockets. He said directly to me, "Where have you been ... old-timer?"

TWENTY-FIVE

A New "Old" Friend

O VER THE NEXT FEW WEEKS, I was taken apart into pieces, just like when I was made in Chicago over half a century ago. The man looked at my serial number and found out that I was the same age as him plus one month. More mystical irony?

My chrome was worked over with a steel wool pad and polished to nearly the same shine as when I was new. My tires and inner tubes were taken off and thrown away. Each spoke was removed and cleaned with steel wool, and my rims were polished to a very high gleam. My old tires were replaced with fancy new whitewalls.

My headlight and taillight were disassembled and polished to a like-new condition and reattached to my handlebars and frame. My pedals were taken completely apart and scrubbed clean, lubricated, and put back together. My handlebars and seat post were also given the steel wool treatment and polished to look like new. All of the shiny parts were like new.

The dents in both fenders were pounded out to look better. My fenders and frame were scratched and rusty, but the man hadn't decided yet whether or not he wanted to repaint me. He said there was something genuine about the character of experience that he may want to hold on to. Every scratch had a story to it. The remaining rust reminded him to take better care of me.

My chain was also so rusted it had to be cleaned with a wire brush. But he was able to get it almost perfect. I was lucky, as I was all original, with no new parts other than my tires and a brand-new bell. He said the bell was "old-school" and fit me just perfect.

He had spent a lot of time cleaning me up and had worked so hard on me. I didn't want to let him down.

TWENTY-SIX

My Second First Ride

FINALLY, THE MOMENT OF TRUTH had arrived. Methodically, slowly, with joyful purpose, my new owner began to put me back together. Every nut and bolt was tightened, and everything that needed oil was oiled. It felt so good. My frame and fenders were cleaned as clean as possible. He applied a light coat of oil on my painted fenders and frame and wiped it dry with a clean cloth.

I had that shine again—not like when I was new, but a definite shine. The radiant green was radiant once more. He adjusted the seat for his height, and the handlebars as well. I was walked down the driveway to the sidewalk, just like I had been when I'd first been ridden by my own young Matthew all those years ago. He turned my handlebars from side to side during the walk to rough up the brand-new whitewall tires.

It was time for my second first ride. He rolled one

of my pedals half a turn forward with his left foot and swung his right leg over the seat and pushed off with his left foot on the pedal. I was moving again!

He was riding me down his block. I could feel every crack in the sidewalk under my new whitewalls and feel the wind once again whistling through my freshly cleaned spokes as we picked up speed. It felt so good! The comforting sound of tires on gravel made that familiar sound that simply cannot be described, except for it being so nostalgic.

His hands were not shaking, but I could feel the excitement in them as he turned into the road to steer me back to the driveway we had started from. He stopped on the side of the street and flipped the switch that put the generator's rotor against my back tire. As we began to move again, my headlight beamed a bright-white light so we could ride safely when the streetlights turned on.

We turned into our driveway as he rang my brand-new old-school bell, and he hit the brakes without skidding as we glided to a stop on the walkway in front of his house. Without even the tiniest squeak, he gently put my kickstand down and ran up the front porch steps and inside to bring his son out to let him see how a great old bike felt to ride.

I saw the years evaporate from the older man as he was telling his son about how it felt to ride me— how it was to hear the gravel and grit grind under the new whitewalls. He talked about how he and his brother use to tinker with old bikes in his garage as a child and how fixing up this old, radiant-green boy's two-wheeler made him feel young again. He recalled many memories and shared them with his son.

His stories were familiar—almost like my stories. For decades, those stories were not thought of or spoken of until he began fixing me up. I knew this, as when he took me apart, I could tell he had done this before.

How lucky I was now. I had a new owner who would appreciate me and use me for what I was intended for. To be ridden and talked about in a good way and be part of creating new memories and new stories—that was my purpose, that's what I was made for.

My new owner may not be a young boy and I may

never hear the words, "Let's race" again. But I can tell you, he sure feels young when he is riding me. And that's good enough for me. I have a new boy again, let's see where we go.

The End

Or a new beginning?